HIGH PLAINS HOSPITALITY

The mountain man was fronted by a hundred of the hardest-cut prairie warriors ever to swing astride a spotted pony.

A flashing burst of pain exploded in the back of his head. The red sun behind Watonga shattered and flew into a thousand pieces . . .

When Jesse came awake, he was tied to a torture stake. This stake was a real *Can Wakan Sha,* a real Red Holy Pole—fifteen feet high, dyed a brilliant scarlet. All doubts a man might have had as to how the Indians intended handling him were pleasantly resolved.

They aimed to barbecue him, North Plains style.

Warbonnet
Clay Fisher

BANTAM BOOKS
TORONTO • NEW YORK • LONDON • SYDNEY • AUCKLAND

WARBONNET

A Bantam Book / published by arrangement with
Clay Fisher

PRINTING HISTORY
Corgi edition published 1961

Bantam edition / December 1970
2nd printing .... April 1971
3rd printing . September 1979
4th printing . September 1985

ISBN 0-553-25318-2

Published simultaneously in the United States and Canada

Bantam Books are published by Bantam Books, Inc. Its trade-
mark, consisting of the words "Bantam Books" and the por-
trayal of a rooster, is Registered in U.S. Patent and Trademark
Office and in other countries. Marca Registrada. Bantam
Books, Inc., 666 Fifth Avenue, New York, New York 10103.

PRINTED IN THE UNITED STATES OF AMERICA

H   13 12 11 10 9 8 7 6 5 4

HISTORICAL FOREWORD

THAT, in the winter of 1853-54, the Mormon leader, Brigham Young, set out to destroy the long-established trading fort of his chief commercial rival and self-appointed personal enemy, fabled mountain man Jim Bridger, is historical fact. That the spiritual head of the Latter-day Saints ever employed any forces other than his own Danite Militia in this undeclared, emigrant-business war will have to remain in the arguable realm of conjecture: irately denied by his supporters, repeatedly and vehemently put forward by his detractors.

In either event, western legend insists that he did. And that the chief and most infamous of these mercenaries was a slab-faced giant of a Wind River Arapaho called Watonga, the Black Coyote.

The author does not mean to imply that this isolated, shadowy incident from the frontier past is in any way representative or typical of the accepted, heroic part of the Mormon Church in the settlement of the West. He writes solely from his private conviction that legend and fact are very nearly synonymous in any standard dictionary of Rocky Mountain History.

CONTENTS

1. JACKPINE SLASH

ANDREW JACKSON HOBBS, nodding over the embers of the nightfire which centered the hollow square of Chouteau & Company's wagon corral outside Fort Laramie, yawned sleepily, cocked a tired professional eye at the rising moon, allowed it must be hard on to ten o'clock.

Judging by the racket from the fort yonder, a man could properly figure his boys wouldn't be home six winks shy of sunup. A man built up a respectable thirst skinning a ten-mule hitch from Kansas City to Fort Laramie up that stinking hot Platte Valley. Apparently his Missouri teamsters were aiming to set a new record in getting rid of theirs. There would be enough trade whiskey spigoted out by morning to float a five-thousand-pound Pittsburgh halfway to St. Louis.

The wagonmaster's ruminations were interrupted by the muffled clip-clopping approach of an unshod horse. Throwing a handful of cottonwood twigs on the embers, the old man squinted across the resulting blaze. What he saw ambling toward him out of the prairie nightblack was the ugliest smoke-grey Indian pony ever foaled. And sitting slack-kneed astride her, what at first glance appeared to be the most ordinary-looking mountain man yet to rig himself out in grease-black buckskins and beaded Sioux moccasins.

Then the cottonwood twigs flared up an extra mite and a man took another look and allowed maybe this jasper wasn't quite as plain as all that.

He sat a horse Indian style, legs hanging straight, body slumped like a sack of wet oats. He was no more than medium tall, wouldn't go over a hundred sixty-five pounds with his shot pouch weighed in. He was clean-shaven, too, which was somewhat for a mountain man, and had the quietest, easiest-looking face a man ever peered into.

Maybe it was that easy, quiet look that fooled you right off, for the next thing you knew you were seeing back of it into the chilliest pair of blue-dark eyes this side of a chunk of lake ice. And then you noticed a couple of other things you had missed. Where he looked on the slight side for a trade that ran to big men, he had a spread of shoulders you could lay an axe haft across. And a set of hands big enough to span a horse pistol, dangling on arms as long and thick as split oak posts. Lastly, as he stepped, quiet-grinning, down off the slat-ribbed pony and into the fire's full light, you caught what in good light would have been the first impression of him.

From where it waved thick and glossy as winter beaver away from his low forehead and back across his small, flat ears to where it tumbled free and shoulder-long to the smoke-dirty collar of his Sioux hunting shirt, his hair was a flaming, wildfire red.

And that gave you your clue, letting you know even before his drawling voice told you so, just who you were looking at. And who you were looking at was, back of maybe only Chris Carson and Jim Bridger themselves, the number-three-mountain man of them all.

"Howdy, mister." The low words carried out the warm promise of the wide-open grin behind them. "I allow you're Andy Hobbs, as is toting Jim Bridger's gunpowder and supplies out from Chouteau's."

"And I allow you're Jesse Callahan, as the Sioux calls the Red Fox," nodded the wagon boss, coming to his feet with the gnarled hand that went out toward the younger man.

"Right as sowbugs under a buffalo chip, Mister Hobbs," grinned the stranger. "How's for a tin of that java before we squat down to cases?"

"Sure thing!" The old man moved quickly to set the black pot among the embers. "And right off, I'll make a deal with you. I aim to call you Jesse, so you mighten as well leave off 'mistering' me."

"It's a deal, Andy. Set the tins out and make yourself cozy. I got news that'll peel your eardrums slicker'n a skinned cat's back."

When Jesse had given the wagonmaster his story, he leaned back with the air of a man who'd just gotten shut of a plenty-hot potato, and who was rightly aiming to have a little fun out of watching some other son juggle it for a spell. Old Andy Hobbs didn't juggle worth a four-bit cussword.

Removing his squat cherrywood pipe, the wagonmaster spat a thin stream of ambeer into the fire. "Well, now, let's see. Near as I can trail you, Bridger's done heard that old

2

Brigham Young over to Deseret* is planning to jump his fort, come snowfall. Also that Brigham had heard about this here shipment of powder and supplies I'm toting out to Bridger's place. And that the cussed Saints has cooked up a deal with some hostile redskins to jump the train and hoist the powder before ever we can get them to Jim's fort. Is that the main of it?"

"That's the main of it," nodded Jesse, grimly. "Old Gabe, that's what us mountain boys calls Bridger, he can't winter it without he gets these supplies, and he can't fight off no Mormon attack without he gets this Du Pont. According, he done sent a Snake scout up to the Three Forks country to locate me."

The grizzled wagonmaster knocked the dottle out of his pipe, peered long and thoughtful into the blackness of the westward-climbing prairie. "Well, I allow this here blow-off twixt Bridger and old Brigham was certain as sunset, right from the beginning."

"I allow it was," agreed Jesse quietly. "Gabe's fort squats square astride the main road, west, and he gets all the emigrant trade right off'n the Mormons' doorstep. The Saints can't stand that, and apparently they don't aim to."

The older man nodded, his words slowing thoughtfully. "Likely you've got a plot of your own for seeing that this Injun, this here 'Watonga' or whatever you called him, gets stopped short of sculpin' the lot of us and liftin' Bridger's Du Pont?"

"Likely I ain't," growled Jesse, shortly. "But I'll tell you this, I ain't yet seen the hostile of his cut that'd jump a full dozen hardcase Missouri skinners, once them rawhide sons was primed and ready for them. You follow me, old salt?"

"Yeah. I only hope you know Watonga better than I do. He's got a trail-riding reputation smellier than a Comanche's blanket."

"I know him all right. We'll bluff the red son clean down to his pigeon toes!"

For the moment, Andy Hobbs only squinted at his red-haired companion, removed his cold pipe, spat doubtfully into the sputtering coals of the fire.

"I sure as tarnal sin hope so, mister!"

The lead-bellied dawn of the next day echoed to some of the most elegant profanity ever barked out by a stumbling

---

* Salt Lake City, the Mormon capital.

dozen, whiskey-sick Missouri skinners. Among the twelve of them, the ory-eyed teamsters hadn't garnered a solid hour's sleep before Andy's harsh screech was bellowing the "Roll outs!" "Catch ups!" and "Stretch outs!" that announced any Oregon Trail outfit's daily taking to the road.

On Jesse Callahan's bobtailed order, the wagon boss put the powder wagon, a spanking new Pittsburgh with sky-blue bed and vermilion wheels, in the middle of the wagon line. Old Andy, jogging grumpily to the bad gait of his ancient saddle gelding, hung back, outriding the last wagon. Out front, fast disappearing in the endless roll of the plains, shuffled the quick-trotting Sioux mare, Heyoka, her rider's restless blue eyes ceaselessly sweeping the western half of the wide prairie compass.

Day after weary and wary day, the train rumbled westward; across Horsehead Creek, over the headlands of La Prell and Deer Creeks, up the ever-rising pull to the North Platte crossing, then on, picking up the headwaters of the East Fork of the Green, and trailing south of that stream toward the Black Fork. A week stretched to two. And on toward three. Then, the seventeenth day, camp was set up at Arapaho Wells, close to the Black Fork—not an unshod pony track or an eagle-feather bonnet tip having been sighted the whole of the tense way.

Sitting over the coals of the wagon-corral fire, along with Andy and the company's boss skinner, Morgan Bates, Jesse broke his long silence.

"Boys, happen you was old Watonga, where would you aim to lay a trap for a red-wheeled goddam* toting six hundred pounds of prime powder?"

The white-haired wagonmaster took the question, shifted his cut plug, shot his customary pre-opinion stream of amber fireward. "First and best spot I know would be Jackpine Slash."

"And where do you place the Slash from this here fire?"

"Half an hour straight downtrail from stretch-out time tomorry morning." Jesse got the short answer from the black-eyed Morgan Bates.

"Percisely," nodded the mountain man, his words picking up, tensely. "Boys, I allow it's time we pulled an Injun-deal on old Black Coyote."

---

* The High Plains Indian word for the huge Pittsburgh and Conestoga freight wagons of the white men.

"Such as what?" Again it was Morgan Bates with the abrupt demand.

"Coyotes is best knowed for sneaking. So we just outsneak old Watonga, that's all." Grinning quietly, obviously enjoying the taciturn attitude of his listeners, Jesse outlined his plan. "Yonder, down south, there, runs an old trace used by the pack-mule outfits in the early forties. Them old boys skun as far around Jackpine Slash as the law'd allow, you can bet. I reckon, happen a man's got mules and guts enough, a wagon can be got over that route. I'm suggesting we douse the cookfires, hitch us a silent hook-up, hit south by moondark and be safe and sound on the far side of the Slash, come broad day."

Andy Hobbs and his boss skinner looked at the scout a long minute. The mountain jasper's idea hung on two maybes: that the Arapaho chief did plan to trap them inside the Slash next day, and that he'd already snuck in and spotted his braves for the try. Maybes or no, neither man had a better hunch, and both accepted Jesse's suggestion with uneasy reluctance.

The moondark hook-up of the mules and the ensuing seven-hour night drive was made without a hitch, the wagons being corralled and the coffee boiled at six the next morning—a safe and solid two miles past the yawning, western exit of Jackpine Slash.

With the coffee downed and the tins hastily rinsed, Jesse made a brief speech.

"Boys," the wide-mouthed grin was working overtime, "we've done got away with murder. Unless I miss my hunch, old Watonga'll be along here directly and feeling meaner than a sorefoot grizzly. I suggest that unless the lot of you have something more pressing than your headpieces to fret about, you all clamber up on them wagon boxes and unwrap your lines. We got forty-three miles to roll to Wild Hoss Bend and I don't aim to let no powder-hunting redskin beat me there!"

Jesse paused after his speech, his slant blue eyes following the sudden scrambling toward their wagons of the impressed skinners. Watching the men, the knifeslash of a grin on his big mouth spread in a split as broad as that of a buffalo wolf's standing over a fresh-killed calf. Andy Hobbs, looking sidelong at the swart-skinned scout, made mental note of what he saw.

This redheaded mountain man had been hostile-Sioux

raised, he knew. And Andy Hobbs reckoned he knew something else, too. Tipi smoke and Indian smell made a powerful strong odor. One that soaked into a man mighty easy. Looking, now, at the hard-eyed trapper, the old wagonmaster allowed quite a bit of that redskin aroma had sunk into the tough hide of close-mouthed, quiet-smiling Jesse Callahan.

Approaching the cold ashes of Chouteau & Company's coffee fire, Black Coyote lowered his rifle, waved his followers to come forward. The clean morning sun put a diamond-bright wash of light around the hostile chief that made him look as big and black as a mountain. And the savage, nomad mind within that gross body was as black and ugly as the mask which covered it. It was thinking now, too, that black mind. Thinking, as the slitted, obsidian eyes trapped and deciphered the telltale corral marks and westward-snaking wheel tracks of the white wagon train.

Followed then, long minutes of prairie stillness during which the Arapaho chief studied the camp signs, and his crowding braves sat their ponies saying nothing. At length Bear Gall, one of the outer warriors, barked, ominously, "What is Watonga thinking? What is to be done, now?"

When a hundred Indians get quiet you can cut it with a wooden knife, it's that thick. The red scores of gargoyle faces turned on Black Coyote, waiting for him to speak. Watonga checked his nervous pinto stud hourse, barked his guttural orders, dead-faced. "Our pemmican is nearly gone. Three days' goddam journey along the river our village waits at the place the *Wasicun* call Piute Crossing. We will go there, and on the way we shall trail this red-wheeled goddam. Maybe I will think of another plan to get that gunpowder. *Hookahey!* Let's go. Let's get out of here!"

The war party swung west along the Fort Bridger road, filling the morning stillness with the ponies' gruntings and with the shuffle-trotting rumble of four hundred unshod hoofs.

2. MEDICINE ROAD

IN camp at Wild Horse Bend, Chouteau & Company's wagon crew washed out the coffee kettle, rinsed the tins, fired up their pipes.

The long reach of timber on Fat Cow Island in midstream of the Black Fork bristled against the red stain of the twilight, harsh as the hairs on an angry dog's back. The foreboding hills across the river crouched still and quiet as so many monster gray cats. Above the subdued mutter of the stream's sharp current, the hushed voices of the teamsters sounded hollow and foreign. The chonk of an axe in a piece of firewood carried half a mile in the heavy silence.

An hour went by, and then another. At nine o'clock, with the prairie nightblack folding in around them close and stuffy as the inside of an old saddlebag, Andy Hobbs told the crew to go ahead and turn in. He and Morgan Bates, quiet smoking, quieter talking, sat the night away, waiting for Jesse Callahan.

From the night three weeks back, when Jim Bridger's red-haired right-hand man had ridden into the wagon corral outside Fort Laramie, Chouteau & Company's white-bearded wagonmaster and his swart boss skinner hadn't known a good night's sleep.

And with perhaps better than a fair-to-middling reason.

When a mountain man of Jesse Callahan's reputation walked his barefoot pony up to your fire and told you that Brigham Young had set a hostile chief of Black Coyote's caliber onto your wagon ruts, you had a mighty good excuse for staying awake nights. At least you did if you knew anything about what a High Plains hostile would do to get his hands on ten pounds of low-grade gunpowder. Let alone on twenty-four full kegs of prime Du Pont. Like, say, those two dozen fat black canisters you had consigned to Fort Bridger in number four wagon, there!

7

Now, stretching into your third week out of Laramie, you hadn't seen so much as an unshod pony track to tell you you were being trailed by the white-hatingest chief on the Medicine Road.* And you were beginning to wonder if Jesse Callahan hadn't been feeding you a mess of trapper's lies about old Brigham and Black Coyote being in cahoots to knock over your supply train and burn out Fort Bridger.

Then at 2.0 a.m., the mountain man rode in. And five minutes after he did, you had all the answer to that last wonder you were likely to need. Happen you were half smart, you did, anyway.

While the wagonmaster stirred up the fire, Jesse chewed a slippery fistful of cold sowbelly, gulped three dippers of cool branchwater. With the edge off his all-day thirst and hunger, the red-haired mountain man wiped the grease from his mouth, made his talk quick and strong.

"Well, they're trailing us, all right. A big bunch, near onto a hundred I'd guess. They've gone into camp back there a few miles. I was late getting back because I wanted to belly-in on them, thinking maybe I could find out why they were laying back instead of being up front setting a trap. Well I didn't find that out but I spotted something else a sight more unsettling."

"Such as?" the dark-faced boss skinner prompted.

"Such as a white man squatting to their smoke cozy as a blood brother. I wasn't so close I could see who it was but he was for sure white and for sure nobody well knowed in these parts."

"Naw!" Morgan Bates was incredulous. "You ain't saying there's a white man other than old Brigham Young mixed up in this deal?"

"I'm saying just that," scowled the mountain man. "And I'll tell you something else I ain't mentioned before. When Bridger told me about Brigham Young hiring Black Coyote to knock off this powder train, and asked me to mosey back to Laramie to guide you into Fort Bridger, he said Washakie, the old Shoshone chief who told him about the Mormon plot in the first place, had warned him there was a strange new white man working between Brigham and the Injuns. Bridger laughed at that and so did I. Injuns will always claim there's a white man to blame for leading other Injuns into trouble."

The narrow-eyed mountain man paused shortly, his hard

---

* The High Plains Indian name for the Oregon Trail.

gaze frosting over. "Well, boys, me, I ain't laughing no more. There *is* a white man steering those red sons."

"Find anything else?" Andy Hobbs frowned the question, like Morgan Bates, not knowing how to figure the full importance of Jesse's discovery.

"Nothing else. But I'll tell you something, boys. Old Watonga, he's got all his top headmen along with him. I seen Yellow Leg, Dog Head, Toad, Blood Face, that lousy little Skull, which is Black Coyote's shadow, and a couple of older chiefs I didn't recognize."

Jesse removed his short stone pipe, spat disgustedly into the fire. "I mean to say that right now I'm smelling more injuns than we've yet seen. And by God I don't cotton none to the stench of them!"

For a long minute, then, the bickering snap of the dry cottonwood twigs and the sibilant hissing of the older coals in the firebed made the only disturbance in the night quiet. Finally, Morgan Bates found a frame for his thoughts.

"I reckon none of us wants to see more hostiles," he muttered, uneasily. "What you aiming to do, Callahan?"

"Push on fast," replied the mountain man. "When I'm smelling them I don't like to squat around with the stink in my nostrils. The wagons ought to roll at five."

"Stopping at Piute Crossing, tomorry?" Andy Hobbs knew they would, but wanted to get a little more out of the taciturn wagon scout.

"Yeah. I'll leave ahead of you, about three. She's moondark the early part of the way, and I'll jog slow. Want to make sure them sons don't get around and flank us again. I had them figured to leave us be once we got here to Wild Hoss Bend, but with them toting that white man along, I don't know. Something's up, likely. It's got me fretted, too. Happen the crazy scuts might yet take their big cut at us."

"Well, you go ahead and have your look, Jesse." The wagonmaster chuckled his head, confidently. "But they ain't going to bother us no more. You'll see."

"I hope so," was all the mountain man said.

And, "You ain't just a-wolfing!" was Morgan Bates's fervent amendment.

Jesse rode slowly, but even so his Sioux mare had him far up the Fort Bridger trail by first light. The scant morning gray let him refresh his remembering of this part of the Fort

Road, quickly showing him it hadn't changed so much as a buffalo chip since the last time he'd covered it. It was an open, desolate country, lonely as a dog wolf crying the sun down back of the Wasatches. What grass there was, was so dry it powdered under a horse's feet like he was walking in a sun-baked puffball bed. The hills on the far side of the Black Fort built themselves rapidly into a regular range, fish-white in color and bare of cover as a mangy hound's head. And withal, high enough to hide all the Arapaho in the Northwest Territory behind the lowest of them.

Why, man, Watonga could be over there a mile away, with half the Arapaho Nation, and not show himself any more than a tumblebug rolling a rabbit berry.

As soon as the sun got up enough to allow a man some far looking, Jesse began spotting distant bands of quick-drifting dust puffs. Antelope, by damn, and him so sick of stringy old mulemeat and sowbelly he could scarce bear it. Still a man wouldn't dast shoot one of the cussed "goats" if it came up and begged him for the favor. In a country like this, where the loudest morning noise was a hawk's shadow chasing a whitefoot mouse through the buffalo grass, a shot would carry most to Deseret and back. One pop out of his Hawken just then would like as not have a man up to his armpits in Arapaho hostiles before the powder smell blew off his buckskins.

Minutes later, with the set of the climbing sun three ponies high over the eastern rim of the prairie to his back, telling a man it was nigh on to seven o'clock, Jesse's "Arapaho nerves" began to cinch down on him in earnest.

It was the cussed glassy-bright daylight that was doing it. There wasn't any Indian, or any bunch of Indians that could get him jumpy so long as he was nightriding. In the pitch-thick starblack that shut down on the High Plains after moonset, one man was as good as a hundred. Especially if the color of your hundred was *red*. The copper-skinned sons, none of them, cottoned to the dark. Their medicine got almighty weak along about sundown, as many another mountain man than Jesse could tell you and, like as not, add that more than a few times he'd owed his nice long hair to the fact.

Now, as Heyoka picked her way gingerly westward, Jesse was thinking of this "dark" chink in the Indian armor. The mountain man grinned frostily, letting his mind run back to Chouteau & Company's wagon camp at Arapaho Wells three nights before Wild Horse Bend. He'd gotten his "nightwork" in there, by cripes, and no two ways about it.

Laying back after the train had rolled on, he'd detoured and slipped back into the Jackpine country from the north to find exactly what he was looking for—enough fresh pony sign along either side of the Slash to tell any hard-grinning mountain man that no less than one hundred unshod Arapaho cayuses had stood the best part of the night away, waiting for Chouteau & Company to deliver Old Gabe's gunpowder to their red owners on daybreak schedule.

Well, the Jackpine Slash run-around had been first blood for Jesse, even if Andy Hobbs and his hard-bitten boss skinner, Morgan Bates, had refused to buy any part of the mountain man's "big pony sign" report. But that had been four days ago—and in the dark. Time enough for a man to have had his grin and get done with it.

Right now there was nothing to grin about. It was broad day and bad country beyond.

Just ahead, now, the prairie rose sharply in a long, swelling ridge, throwing a five-mile, north-south earthen dike athwart the westerly running tracks of the wagon road. And cutting a man's view of the country beyond, sharp off. With or without the rise, Jesse didn't need to top that ridge to know what lay west of it—it was five miles of the best ambush land old Man Above had ever laid out for his fun-loving little red sons.

If Watonga was looking for a proper place to cover up the pony droppings he'd left in Jackpine Slash, this was it.

Jesse reckoned he had two moves open—he could wait for Andy and the wagons, figuring to drive on through with the Pittsburghs and make a head-on fight of it, or he could go on in alone, now, figuring to smell out the trap and maybe drive around it again. One way it was risking Gabe's good black powder, the other, his own fine red hair.

The rim-ice of the grin put its fleeting frost once more to the wide lips. Well, one thing was sure as the price of snow was low in the Sierras. He wasn't getting paid to pamper his topknot. The Sioux hunting moccasins hammered into the surprised ribs of the loafing Heyoka. With a grunt the gray mare swung back into her stride, answering the demand of the driving heels, pointing her ugly jughead straight west along the wandering wagon track.

Up and over the rise Jesse put the mare, letting her take her head and pick her own gait down the falling path of the road beyond the ridge. The thing to do in a blind ride-up like

11

this was to play it easy-like and straight in—to make out like there wasn't a blessed thing in the wine-clear of the Wyoming morning to put a trail-wise mountain man on edge—to let Watonga and whichsoever of his boys as might be waiting in those gully-slashed hills, up yonder, get the feeling that Jesse Callahan figured he'd broken their red hearts with that fancy-dan nightdrive around Jackpine Slash.

At the same time a man needn't let any such mushy notions take root under his own headpiece. Leastways, not if he wanted to keep wearing it.

Jesse's slant gaze quartered the waiting stillness of the cutup country ahead, wary as a loafer wolf moving upwind into a baited buffalo carcass. The lightning, nervous stab of the narrow blue eyes missed nothing, yet the burnished sheen of the long hair seemed scarcely to move. It was a High Plains art, painstakingly taught him by his Sioux foster parents, this trick of quartering or even halving the prairie compass with the eyes, while the head itself remained still, and right now Jesse Callahan was practicing that art for all it was worth.

Still he saw nothing. No least sign that read wrong.

That painted speck of a hawk yonder, motionless against the harsh blue sky, was hanging just right. He wasn't hunting. He wasn't worried. Just sitting up there, quiet and happy. Had there been men below him, unless uncommon well hid and death's-head still, old Wanbli K'leska would have been swinging wide and low, wheeling silently in the broad, restless arc of the watch-flight.

The service-berry birds, flitting the snowflash of their stern feathers thick as cotton blossoms in the matted brush ahead, were carrying on their high-voiced banter as though the only human in Southern Wyoming Territory was the lone white rider there heading in from the east.

The wind, full in Jesse's face, brought no slightest taint of sweated pony flesh, nor of naked, redskin rider-smell. The mountain man could make that much out by watching Heyoka's ears as the little Sioux mare worked the morning breeze with her sooty nostrils. Had there been enemy horseflesh within as much as a mile, those ears would have been as sharp-pointed as twin Bowie blades.

Well, a man could read right-sign all day and still lose his scalp if he was pigheaded enough to ignore his Indian-nerves.

The hills were reaching out for him and Heyoka now, and the mare, all on a sudden, was cat-jumpy and skitter-stepping. Jesse clamped her fast with the iron bow of his long legs, sat down on her, short and hard, with the braided hackamore rope. She steadied somewhat but her eyewhites were rolling, now, and Jesse allowed she was spooked for sure.

Thirty seconds later they were deep between the first of the hill shadows. Five seconds after that, Jesse saw two things in the same split instant—the final, right-swinging set of Heyoka's ears—the death-sudden warning of the sun-flashing rifle barrels.

The mountain man and the mare parted company on the dead run, Jesse rolling off her offside as she bolted past a shoulder-high outcrop of sheltering granite, the Sioux pony bombarding on up the Medicine Road like a tail-shot doe. Jesse hit the ground behind the outcrop, taking the fall on his shoulder so that the precious Hawken might not take on any muzzle dirt. He rolled twice and came to a hard stop in a choke of service-berry bushes and piled boulders, acting just as dead as any jasper ought to be who'd let himself in for a broad daylight belly-shoot by a handful of Watonga's mangy coyotes.

There'd been no more than three of the sons. Leastways, no more than three had let drive at him if he'd counted the shots right. They'd been dug-in on the wide-open flank of the left-hand hill, just about the last spot you'd aim to expect them from. That would explain them foxing old Wanbli and the service-berry birds. They'd no doubt come in before daylight, roughed out their rifle pits, spread themselves over with dry brush and not breathed deep enough to rustle a grass-tip since sunup. Another thing for sure: since Heyoka hadn't winded any ponies, the red scuts must be afoot.

In the three seconds it took these pictures to flash against the desperate plate of Jesse's mind, the mountain man had thought of and discarded one plan, made and held to another.

A man's first hunch, once he knew they were afoot and only three-strong, was to roll right on up and to down the first one that broke cover with the Hawken, leaving it to trapper's luck to somehow outdodge the other two. But happen all three of them jumped and came down on him at once, he'd have thrown his first lead at long range and left two of the sons free to pin him down till the main bunch could come up.

Jesse had to allow he'd made a pretty good tumble off that

13

mare. Had to figure it was even good enough to fool most redskins. Gambled, now, that the next seconds would bring all three of his Arapaho friends busting over the near-edge of the outcrop, scrambling, hog-eager, to see who would be the first to put his knife back of the downed scout's ear and lift that handsome red scalplock.

The thought no sooner formed than the pulse-thudding race of moccasined feet sounded across the dust-puddled surface of the wagon road. Jesse grinned, gathering his long thighs beneath him, cradling the Hawken short-up, swinging its octagonal black snout across the eight-foot distant crest of the outcrop. Happen the next handful of seconds went just right, three of Black Coyote's best boys were due to find out they'd ought never to come in, arm-close, on a downed mountain man.

His handful of seconds fell jarringly into place. One. Two. Three. The copper-dark forms hurtled over the outcropping to land in a whirling crouch, their slit eyes and ocher-painted faces swinging in darting search of their disabled quarry.

The first Arapaho probably never saw his "wounded" enemy. For the elemental reason that not even a seasoned buck can make out much without eyes. Jesse's shot took him full in the panting mouth, the heavy .50-caliber slug angling upward from the ground to rip through the roof of the mouth and take along the entire top of the head, including the upper half of the face. The second tribesman fared a little better. He saw Jesse. Saw the long form of the mountain man rising from the ground. Saw the momentary hang of the long rifle barrel in its driving flight toward his groin. Felt the searing pain burst behind his bulging eyes, and saw no more, his tortured body thrashing blindly to the ground in a shockburst of unbearable pain. The third savage saw even more. As a matter of fact, had time to see enough to get his scalping-knife arm drawn back to strike at the snarling Jesse. Even time to unleash its whistling cut toward the turning form of the mountain man. And with that, his time ran out.

Jesse caught the knifeblow on the crossheld length of his Hawken's barrel, the Indian's muscular forearm striking the heavy barrier with bone-snapping force, the scalping knife whirling harmlessly from the spasming fingers. Then Jesse was into him, whipping his own thin blade from its hanging neckthong, twisting behind him, barring his corded left forearm across the Arapaho's throat, leaving his right arm free to put the steel where it would do the most good—in the

14

lower small of the straining back, just behind the soft kidney fat and above the hard rim of the pelvis.

The mountain man stepped back, letting the stricken Indian stagger past him and buckle saggingly to his knees. Jesse watched him a moment, closed-eyed, nodded abruptly, turned away. That one would last three minutes. Maybe five. They bled inside from those kidney cuts. Went out quickly and easy, with not much pain. Not anything like a bowel slash or a muscle cut.

As Jesse turned, now, to retrieve his Hawken, the second hostile was beginning to show agonized signs of life. Again the white scout nodded. Nothing like a groin double-up to down a man and take his mind off of premeditated murder, but in the cob-rough roster of frontier fighting techniques it was by no means as well held as a rifle slug in the roof of the mouth or a skinning blade through the base of the kidney.

This one would live to bear the bad news back to Watonga.

Jesse kicked the groaning savage's knife away, dragged him, unresisting, to his feet. He had to hold him, back-wedged to the outcropping, to keep him from slumping. "*Iho!* Well, now!" The harsh Sioux gutturals brought a flicker of understanding from the pain-darkened eyes. "What are you called? What is your name?"

"*Pizi*, Bear Gall," the sufferer's answer came in halting Sioux, "and I have had enough. I want to die, now."

Jesse nodded grimly, well able to understand that part of it. He stepped back, releasing Bear Gall. "Not just yet, cousin. All in good time." The captive's eyes reflected his surprise at the continuing softness of the mountain man's voice. "Now you are free. Now you may go. Back to Black Coyote, you understand?" As he talked, watching the Indian's reactions, he was swiftly ramming and priming the Hawken.

The Arapaho nodded dumbly, not yet able to comprehend the quality of mercy in an enemy who fought with the fury of this redheaded *Wasicun*.

Jesse eyed him, letting his words fall slowly. "Now you are to tell him who has done this to you and your brothers. You are to tell him it was Tokeya Sha." The mountain man saw the slit eyes widen, and queried innocently. "What is it, cousin? You have heard the name?"

"Tokeya, the Minniconjou? Tokeya Sha, the Red Fox?" There was that in the way the lean warrior phrased the names, paying them just the proper compliment of impressed disbelief, that let Jesse know Black Coyote's wasn't the only name of doubtful reputation running the campfire gamut of the North Plains.

"The same," he nodded soberly. "Do you think you can remember it?"

"Aye—long enough."

"*Nohetto!*" snapped Jesse, suddenly and for no good reason nervous again. "There you are, then. That's all. Go, now!"

The Arapaho turned without a word, starting eastward along the wagon road. As Jesse watched him, he paused, flicking his hand toward the looming hill on the white scout's right. "*Ha ho,*" he called in Sioux, "thank you," and then, unaccountably, in Arapaho, "*Ni'-inaei,* good hunting. Don't close your eyes yet, cousin." With that, he was gone, limping into the hill shadows, leaving Jesse to puzzle over the strange character of his parting words and outflung gesture. Then the mountain man had it. That little handwave to the hill, yonder. The odd phrase, "Don't close your eyes yet, cousin." Cripes! The red son had been warning him!

Jesse dropped behind the outcrop the instant the thought came home, the ugly whine of the half-ounce lead ball splattering the granite inches over his red head, telling him the Arapaho had just returned him a slight favor. Oh, nothing much. Nothing a white man not raised by Indians would understand. Just a little thing. A matter of common courtesy. A life for a life. *He-hau,* no more than that.

This time Jesse had no thought of playing prairie possum. In the first place that shot had come from near the top of the same hill the Arapaho had been staked out on, and it had been a long, long shot, too, judging from the delay between the bullet's arrival and that of its report's discharge. In the second place the sound of that discharge, itself, had been all wrong. Too flat and harsh for one of the hollow-booming old smooth-bore trade muskets in main use among the hostiles. That was a Hawken's crack if a man'd ever heard one. And it had been bare inches shy of knocking his head off at near on to five hundred yards!

Mister, Indians just didn't hold that close.

Jesse slid the Hawken's barrel around the end of the outcrop while the bouncing echoes of his would-be assassin's shot were still growling away from the farther hills. His answering shot, taken from the ground and without shouldering his piece, was a pure snap—and a good, clean miss.

Nevertheless, it threw up a shower of rotten granite chips a scant foot behind the scuttling figure just diving over the skylined crest of the hill.

Five hundred yards is no distance to be fooling with in any offhand hurry, that was for sure as stale grease stank. Neither for clear sniping, nor for clean seeing. Howsomever, happen that big, tousle-haired buck that'd just dusted over the crest yonder was a Arapaho, Jesse would put in with you. There might be a few things the mountain man didn't know about his High Plains homework but Indians wasn't one of them.

In the suspended stillness following his return shot, and as if in confirmation of the thought forming in his mind, the freshening west wind now brought to the scout's ear the diminishing drumfire of sudden-spurred hoofbeats. They echoed dully from beyond the hill, rang sharply out as the fleeing animal passed over a stretch of exposed rock, faded and were gone.

Jesse cursed silently. Turned to whistle up the Sioux mare who, her first breakaway gallop quickly run out, had fallen to peacefully cropping the short grass of the Medicine Road's wagon ruts. Tote it anyway you wanted, when you added up that kiss-close, five-hundred-yard shot, plus the shod-hoof ring of his quick mounted getaway, you came up with one, deadsure answer.

That'd been a *white* man up there.

3. BLACK FORK CROSSING

By ten o'clock the smooth-walking Heyoka had covered sixteen miles, bringing the mountain man within long sight of that night's wagon camp at Piute Crossing of the Black Fork.

The burned-out frontier post at this spot had always been an interesting place to Jesse, and what he spied when he got up on it this time did nothing to dull that interest.

At the site of the gutted log walls, the southbank hills threw a spur of their range over onto the north side of the Fork. This wing of hills sheltered a good grove of big pines and cottonwoods, protecting them from prairie fire wipe-out and letting them survive to furnish firewood, sunshade and storm shelter to the Trail traffic. The crumbling walls of the old post made a handy breastwork to get back of in case of an Indian attack, and the cool Black Fork ran close by, with its bottom meadows thick with excellent forage grasses. It was the favored campsite of the old Fort Bridger road—of both white and red traveler.

In this case, what intrigued the narrow-eyed Jesse was that it was being favored by *both* colors!

Even at that distance, the mountain man could see that the white outfit was an emigrant outfit, and a poor one. Their shoddy wagons were corralled around the ancient log walls about as sloppy as any outfit's could be, their cookfires and camp rig scattered around *outside* the protecting timbers.

The red camp was something else. Or it would be once the Indians, now methodically rearing their lodges, got it set up. And for a spell of years thereafter, certain surviving members of that shabby white caravan were going to be blessing the fact that Jim Bridger's close-mouthed protégé and hastily appointed supply-train chaperon rode into their lives when he did—which was in good time to see those *Shacun* lodges going up. And to read from the number of lodgepoles employed in the tipi frames and the distinctive markings of

18

the buffalo hide coverings their exact tribal identity: northern Wind River Arapaho!

Jesse watched the Indians for a string of long minutes, saw they were intent on setting their village straight, knew from that, and the absence of picketed war ponies close in, that they were planning no immediate trouble for the whites.

Putting Heyoka to a stiff lope, he sent the smoke-gray mare up the Fork bottoms, keeping her down behind the shelving banks which buttressed the stream at this point. When he got upstream past the old log walls, he turned the mare into the heavy timber of the grove, came silently down behind the straggling white camp.

Midway through the grove an old channel of the Fork, cut there by some forgotten year's high water, protruded from the main channel like a probing finger feeling back into the woods. After a wet spring like the past one, this side channel held a trap of backwater well through summer. Called Piute Slough, this sometimes wilderness pool made a perfect spot for secluded bathing, particularly welcome to pioneer white womenfolk who had likely been on the trail many a dusty day's drive from Fort Laramie without any other such God-made grove to hide their ablutions.

With Heyoka stepping neat and dainty as a cat, Jesse came up to the slough without being seen—but not without seeing. And what he was seeing was six white women bathing in Piute Slough. Six full-grown emigrant females as delightfully unclad as the day the merciful Lord had delivered them. And with nothing between them and the happily surprised Jesse but a lacy-thin screen of clean-leaved cottonwoods!

The mountain man's little Sioux mare accepted the bracing sight as quickly and favorably as did her approvingly head-cocked rider. Heyoka's ears went forward and she got her nostrils flared for a good, friendly snort. And that was all she got. Jesse clamped his paw on her snout before the impending greeting got halfway down the Roman nose. Muzzle-wrapping the sociable mare with a sharp turn of the hackamore, the trapper slid his buckskinned leg over her crouching rump and stepped noiselessly to the ground. Only after that did he grant himself the pleasure of a silent whistle of plumb-center appreciation.

Man Above! Now wasn't that a scandalous, noisy, jaybird carrying-on of chattering and splashing for you? And mustn't a man rightly allow they looked just as fresh and pretty as they sounded, the clean-swimming grace of their bodies all shimmery white and exciting through the clear green wash of the sloughwater? The momentary man-grin of Jesse's immediate appraisal faded as the slower more sober workings of his mind caught up with the unquestioned quickness of his eye, its happy place swiftly taken by a downcast, brow-furrowed frown of real thought.

A man sort of got women out of his head living the life Jesse Callahan had been living these past lonely years. Seeing these white womenfolk got his thoughts to again, moving to his own restless and uncertain future. Jesse was plenty agey enough to start figuring on a female and maybe even young ones of his own. These women made him remember that, hard sudden. Made him remember that for all his seamy life and lonely, wild ways, what Jesse Callahan wanted more than anything, more than his share of all that gold in California, was a real woman of his own color. A white-skinned one, you could bet, and light-haired. One with real blue eyes. That was his idea of a woman, by cripes—one with yellow hair and blue eyes.

Right now, though, he wasn't seeing any in that bunch beyond the cottonwoods that seemed to fit his bill. And besides, the whole bunch of them were having such a proper time of it yelling and splashing each other with so much honest ginger it couldn't help but take a man's mind back to what he was supposed to be doing there.

And what he was supposed to be doing there wasn't blundering up on and stampeding a trail-worn passel of middle-aged women taking themselves a decent bath!

Jesse backed away from the slough brush, hand-leading the mare, careful to put his feet so as not to startle the bathers with any twig-poppings. Once well away from the cottonwood clump he swung up on Heyoka and began walking her on around the slough. He had gone perhaps sixty yards, coming to the inland end of the water, when he saw her.

Maybe if the good Lord had set it up otherwise, a lot of things might not have happened. A red-wheeled Pittsburgh full of gunpowder might have wound up in Fort Bridger where it belonged. Jesse Callahan might have gone on wandering around the Rockies until he was as old and kneesprung as Andy Hobbs. And Watonga might have headed for home with a full hide of hair and an unsmoked reputation.

But the Man Upstairs had it in mind otherwise.

She was sitting on a sandbar at the far edge of the slough,

maybe fifty feet from the staring mountain man. She had been bathing and had been out of the water just long enough for the wandering softness of the prairie air to get into her hair and begin to fluff it out. And, mister, that was some hair to get into!

Yellow as July cornsilk, it flooded down over her shoulders clean to her full-curving hips, and the way she was reclining it covered a lot a man might otherwise admire to see. Maybe a mite more, even, than he would the hair.

She had her long legs drawn up under her, her body sort of angled forward to the slant of the sun, and that way about all a man could make out of her was that she was next thing to full naked, the damp-sheer cling of the flimsy camisole doing its level, transparent best to wantonly wetmold every bold-wicked body curve it so mockingly proposed to cover. Jesse, the blood-race pumping his head till his temples were near bursting with the hammer of it, let his slant eyes narrow with the hungry wish she would move a mite.

Obligingly, she did.

Stretching slowly, she brought her arms up to brush the golden wave back where it properly belonged. She had been crouching on an old piece of buffalo robe and now she lay back on it with a sinuous ease and smoothness that minded Jesse of nothing so much as a big, slim cat sprawling out to sun-soak. But apparently she had lain back only to stretch, for after a heart-thumping minute that had Jesse's stomach wrapped three ways around his backbone, she rolled to her knees and stood up.

Then for the first time you really saw all of her.

She was tall, five-ten, anyway, Jesse guessed, and a pure cross between a cat and a young willow for slender, moving grace. But the slender part of it went only as far as it should. Like to the waist, the slim wrists and ankles, the tapering hands, small feet and clean, straight knees. Otherwise, what she was supposed to have was where she was supposed to have it. And it was there with a saucy, firm-sculptured authority scarce challenged by the full, warm-damp embrace of the freshly wet camisole.

That the mountain man could have remained unannounced party to much more of this inadvertent peep-tomming will have to remain in the realm of the highly improbables. Fortunately, the young woman took this moment to turn with her retrieved camp dress over her arm, looking for the first time across the slough.

In accidentally riding up on the emigrant woman, Heyoka had carried Jesse out of the covering brush. For the full term of his wonder-struck preview, the red-haired trapper had sat there in plain view, fat and stupid as a tickbird on a bull buffalo's back.

The girl didn't waste any effort screaming, she just went diving behind the nearest brush clump, immediately popping her head back over the top of it. There she poised herself, wide-eyed and motionless, waiting for the stranger to speak.

A man couldn't help liking that, too—her not yapping like a stepped-on puppy just because a strange man had seen her in her underclothes. Most women would still have been ki-yi-ying about it. There was another thing he liked, too. Something he hadn't noticed about her until she'd gotten clean behind that cussed brush: her face, by Tophet!

Breaking out his best set of teeth, Jesse flashed her a spreading grin. "Mornin', ma'am. Trust I didn't startle you. I didn't aim to ride up on you thisaway." As he talked, he watched her face, liking it better every second.

He'd always cottoned to high-cheekboned women with thin nostrils and short, straight noses. If those noses turned up a midge on the end, like this one, he didn't mind that, either. At the same time, he liked a good jaw on a girl. And a full, wide mouth. And above all, a juicy lower lip that pouted out a mite like hers was doing, right now.

"You frightened me, all right, mister." The voice had just enough satin in it to go right with the face and figure. "What do you want?"

"What's your name, ma'am?" Jesse ignored her question to put his own.

"Lacey. Lacey O'Mara."

"*O'Mara*—" He let his tongue curl around the name like a kid slurping blackstrap off a bent pewter spoon. "Lacey O'Mara! Sure, now, the whole thing's the luck of the Irish, ma'am. Mine's *Callahan*. Jesse Patrick Callahan!"

For the first time the girl's face relaxed. Jesse had thought he'd thrown her a real dazzler with that smile of his; he abruptly discarded his whole previous scale of smile-values. He had never seen a real smile before. He practically had to squint his eyes shut, to bear the way the sun bounced off her white teeth. "That's fine, Mister Jesse Patrick Callahan, but I'm not Irish and you're not in luck. That 'O'Mara' didn't come with me. I picked it up along the way. It's *Mrs.* O'Mara to you, mister!"

Jesse clucked to Heyoka.

The little mare stepped into the slough, started chopping through the shallows toward the hiding girl. "It's all right, ma'am," the mountain man called, noticing the alarm which straightened the smile-curve of her mouth. "I'm just coming over to see the color of your eyes."

When he had reined Heyoka out the far side, the girl found her voice. "You bring that awful little horse one step closer and I'll scream bloody murder."

"This is close enough," breathed Jesse, studying her frowning face. "Glory to Heaven, ma'am, they're pure blue!"

"What are? What are you talking about?"

"Your eyes, ma'am. They're bluer than a South Dakota sky, and that's somewhat. I allow they had to be, too, ma'am. Seems I just knowed that all along."

"Look, I don't know what you mean, mister, and I don't care. But you go right away, this minute, or I'm going to start yelling."

"Wait a minute, Mrs. O'Mara—" The girl, catching the earnestness in his plea, checked her shout. "I'll ride along but I just want to say this—" His eyes bored into hers, making her drop her gaze, blush hotly, feel, all at once, the hard-framed man of him. "I always said that if ever I found the woman I wanted, and she had blue eyes, Old Nick couldn't get that water of his high enough to keep me away from her. Well, ma'am, I've found her and her eyes are just as blue as a man could dream."

She didn't answer, keeping her lashes downswept. When she did raise her head, he was still sitting there.

"Goodbye, Lacey—" The blue-eyed, prairie-burnt look of him ran down her spine, chilling her whole body with its excitement. "I'll see you again."

He was gone after that, jogging his ugly gray pony toward the old fort walls, leaving her in mouth-parted silence.

Lacey O'Mara gasped. The nerve of him! The sheer gall! Sitting and watching her walk around half naked then quietly telling her he was going to have her, hell or high water—mainly, to judge from his laconic remarks, because her eyes were blue! Hah! Well, the world was full of strange people and he was a relief, anyway. Not many had his clean, fierce look and easy, straight way of talking.

She watched the tall ramrod of his figure going toward the timber, sitting the little horse like an Indian, long legs dangling straight down. There was plenty in those wide shoulders, hanging red hair, narrow sun-black face and piercing eyes to excite far less hungry women than Lacey O'Mara.

He was just another man, though, for all his hard good looks and outlandish buckskin fringes. If you were a woman as old as Lacey, you had to remember that. You couldn't let yourself get to thinking about any man when you were thirty years old and had two kids of your own. Two kids and a bad lot like Tim O'Mara for your husband.

Nonetheless, she was still looking at Jesse when he checked the mare short of disappearing in the timber. Wheeling Heyoka, he called softly back, "Ma'am, you get them other women and come on into camp. It's the Injuns, ma'am, but don't scare them up about it. Just hustle them on in."

She nodded, waving a bare arm in reply. He waved back, turning the horse out of sight behind the screening cottonwoods.

When Jesse rode into the emigrant camp, he found the menfolk gathered around the ashes of the morning cookfire. They were a seedy, whipped-hound bunch if a man ever saw one. The kind of an outfit, Jesse allowed, that God spent his off nights sitting up looking after.

He came to them without giving any greeting or getting any. Swinging off Heyoka, he dropped the hackamore rope to the ground and went in long, bent-kneed strides toward them.

"Howdy—" His lean, square-shouldered figure in its grease-blackened buckskins and loose belt of blazing Sioux beadwork worked in sharp contrast to the slovenly homespuns, flat hats and crude cowhide boots of his listeners. "I'm Jesse Callahan, as works for Jim Bridger up to the fort."

"Howdy," a couple of men mumbled replies, not bothering to get up with them. The rest sat and stared, saying nothing.

"Who's in charge?" Jesse demanded, his eyes not liking what he saw of these scarecrows, his knowledge of the Medicine Road telling him their story before they had a chance to.

"Tim is, I guess," one of them vouchsafed. "Leastways he says he is."

"Tim who?" Jesse asked, confining his question to the man who had answered him.

"O'Mara," the other grunted.

"Well, which one of you is O'Mara?"

24

"He ain't here," said the spokesman.

"Where is he?" queried Jesse, shortly.

"Around, somewheres—"

"Well? And where might 'around somewheres' be, mister?" Jesse was beginning to get nettled with the plumb-dumb attitude of the emigrants.

"Nappin' over yonder under one of the wagons, I reckon. Leastways, I think I see'd him beddin' down over there half an hour ago when he come in off his mornin' scout ride. 'Course I wouldn't know."

"You don't appear to know much," nodded Jesse, turning his back on them. "O'Mara! Where are you? Sing out." The mountain man threw his call toward the wagon the other man had indicated, and got his answer in a surly growl from behind the canvas-draped wheels.

"Over here where you was told, trapper. What's it to you?"

Jesse thought that over. It stumped him enough so that he hunkered down with the others to await the pleasure of Mr. O'Mara's early morning siesta. Meanwhile, he fired questions at the hollow-cheeked men, and got enough answers to add up to what he had already figured.

The group was made up of emigrant land-seekers from east Kansas territory, around Shawnee. They had banded together and headed west with eight ox-wagons. They had been California-bound, and had gotten up the Trail as far as Fort Bridger with fair luck and no bad Indian scrapes.

Jesse had nodded, understanding that last part of it. No self-respecting Sioux or Cheyenne, much less any high-caste Arapaho, would bother a scrubby bunch like these.

At Fort Bridger the outfit had found themselves dangerously low on funds, had listened to the friendly advice of Jim Bridger and turned back for the settlements. The old mountain man had pointed out to them the lateness of the season, the poor condition of their wagon stock and the good chance of their running into a fatal snowtrap in the distant Sierras. Jesse could understand that, too, and it made real sense.

When the emigrants had voted to turn back, Tim O'Mara, their hired guide, had refused to head back with them, saying he had business that wouldn't keep, waiting for him in Salt Lake. They had paid him off and he had taken out for the Mormon capital alone, abandoning his woman and young ones, who for some reason, refused to go with him.

The emigrants had pulled into Piute Crossing the night

before Jesse found them. But it was only this very morning, just after the Arapaho village had arrived, that Tim O'Mara had suddenly and unaccountably shown up again, saying only that his affairs in Salt Lake were in hand and that he was offering to guide them back to Shawnee without wages.

At this point in the discussion, Tim O'Mara came slouching out of his wagonbed boudoir. One eyetail look at him and Jesse knew he had his hands full.

Tim was a big man, far bigger than Jesse. He was that kind of a bear of a man the Irish sometimes breed. Hefty, ham-handed, a meatslab of a face, rough-handsome a few years back, now coarsening up fast. Small eyes, hot-tempered, not smart. A bad man sober, a pure grizzly, drunk.

"Howdy," Jesse nodded. "I'm Jesse Callahan."

"Yeah, I heard your big mouth going. What do you want?"

"Looks like you could use some help. Leastways, your folks can. Maybeso I can give it to you."

"We ain't got any money." The statement wasn't an apology, it was a challenge, and Jesse knew the big emigrant was watching him, sizing him up fightingwise.

"I said *give* it to you," the mountain man replied, careful to see that his words came out without flavor, one way or the other.

"You mean *guide* for us? Huh! I guess we know the way by this time. Backwards, anyway. We just come over it."

"I didn't say *what* I meant," announced Jesse, slowly, "but I'm aiming to if—"

"Why don't you climb your hoss, mister?" The big man's interruption was harsh. "We've had all the trouble we need and we ain't lost no squawman in buckskins and Injun shoes. Go on, get moving!" With the words, O'Mara moved toward the mountain man, the glint in his pig eyes saying clear as glass that he'd be mainly pleased if Jesse didn't aim to accommodate his order.

The red-haired trapper stood up easy and cautious. He'd seen his share of Tim O'Maras, handled them as they came along. You didn't talk to a slob like that. Leastways, not with your mouth.

Tim stopped two steps away, feet braced, tiny eyes pinning Jesse's noncommittal glance. "You getting on that hoss by yourself, little man, or is Tim O'Mara boosting you up?"

26

The other men were finding their feet, moving away from the fire.

"Help yourself," said Jesse quietly, and made his move.

None of the bystanders saw how that Hawken's butt got switched around in the mountain man's hands, much less Tim O'Mara. But they all heard the grunt that exploded out of the hulking Irishman as the rifle stock drove itself halfway to the trigger guard in the hard fat of his belly. Tim doubled forward, covered his stomach, stumbling toward Jesse. The mountain man side-stepped as he came, letting him fall past him, the rifle swinging in another blurred arc as he did. The crack of the barrel steel on Tim's thick skull sounded like a double-bit axe bouncing off an elm burl.

"Prop him against that wheel," Jesse directed, "and slosh him with that can of coffee water."

A belt on the head with a rifle barrel will slow a bear down. When he came around Tim stayed where he was, sagged against the wagon wheel, listening sullenly to Jesse's talk. While the latter was having his say, the womenfolk, returned from the slough, drifted up to stand gray and silent behind their men.

"The first thing," the mountain man began, "is that Injun camp, yonder. They're meaning you some trouble, or I don't know red skin when I see it. Soon as I'm done talking to you, I'll mosey over there and palaver with them. See can I get a line on their aims and ambitions as regards you folks. Meanwhile, I want you should listen close to what I've got to say.

"I got a twelve-wagon freight outfit due in here this afternoon. With them spanned out around you, you'll be safe for right now. But I got to roll them wagons on up to Fort Bridger. We can't lay over here at all. Now, if you're smart you'll tag on up to Gabe's fort with us, then hook up with a strong outfit heading east. Next to that, you can wait right here until one comes through, eastbound. But on no account should you head east alone. I've just had some trouble with a strong bunch of Arapaho back yonder where you're bound for. They're regular trail raiders and spoiling for any kind of bait, right now. We whipped their tails off'n them, the way that Injuns look at such things, and I allow the next white outfit they see will get charged for the lesson. I advise you not to let it be yours."

"Mister," the man named Tom Yarbrough, the one who had spoken to Jesse before, answered him, "I believe you. We should ought to do what you say. But hang it all, we can't.

We ain't got the food, nor the extry draft cattle, no more. If we head on right away, we might just last it out to Shawnee. We ain't got no choice, mister. We got to go on back."

Tim, his wits unscrambling gradually, was watching the talk now. Not looking at Jesse, he grunted an obscene agreement with Tom Yarbrough's objections. Encouraged, the other men began speaking up, testily. Jesse, seeing he was licked for the minute and hoping he could get the emigrants to listen to Andy Hobbs when the powder train got in, broke up the meeting.

"All right, we'll leave it the way it is till my wagons get in. Then we can put the whole thing up to the Company wagonmaster. He's been with the Chouteaus for thirty years, and working this Oregon Road for the past five of that time. I allow you'd listen to him where likely you wouldn't to me."

Several of the men nodded. Jesse looked at Tim O'Mara, waiting for him to speak. "What do you say, Tim?" he asked, finally. "You willing to talk it again, tonight? When Hobbs and the Company outfit gets here?"

The burly emigrant got up, bracing his back along the wheel to let himself make it. When he stood, he swayed a little before his legs steadied. A thin trickle of blood was seeping from his nostrils, a blue lump the size of a horsecollar gall growing behind his left ear.

His eyes, beginning at the ground, ran slowly up Jesse's leggin's and across his hunting shirt, coming to rest squinting full on the mountain man's dark face. His tongue ran over his upper lip, clearing it of the blood. His words, along with the blood and spittle, were spat viciously into the ground at Jesse's feet.

"You can kiss my foot, squawman. I'm through talking."

When he walked away, the flushed women parted to let him through, the white-faced men going awkwardly back to their staring into the sifting cookfire ashes. A pin, dropped in the ankle-deep dust of the campground, could have been heard in Kansas City.

For an hour Jesse lay resting in the noonshade of the outer emigrant wagon, watching the activity in the Indian camp across the meadow.

It never ceased to amaze him the way these red nomads would move in on a chunk of sagebrush and make a city of it in sixty minutes. This bunch was no exception. Every lodge had its assigned place in the Pitching Plan, carried its own coverskins, poles, floor robes and sleeping furs. Even as Jesse watched, the tipis sprang up like dirty brown mushrooms, growing in a dopa, or square, of four groups of lodges centered around an open middle square. This central square was the dance and council grounds, the middle space always reserved for the communal palavers and various ceremonial stomps forever taking place in any High Plains village.

The mountain man waited until the last lodge-skin was in place and the older Indian boys had started scattering the vast pony herd out along the riverbanks to graze. Then he took a look at the pan of his rifle, eased the Sioux skinning knife in its sheath and stepped up on the dozing Heyoka.

Riding toward the camp, he was struck by two things: the abnormal quiet of the red village, and its respectable size. The first, a man would know from his vivid memories of the usual pandemonium of squealing children, strident-voiced squaws and yapping camp curs which provided the audible atmosphere of the average plains village, particularly one which had just been set up. Among these tall, smoke-stained lodges, even the dogs seemed to move in unnatural and skulking silence. The second, any mountain man could gather by counting his fingers five times. There were fifty lodges of the red sons and putting the prairie rule of thumb to that number (five Indians to the lodge) you came out with about two hundred and fifty Arapaho.

The minute Jesse had noted, from his first sight of this village, that it was a Wind River band, he had thought of the warrior pack of the same tribe which had attempted to waylay Old Gabe's supply train in Jackpine Slash. This village was just of a size to be Watonga's, for the same rule of thumb that gave you five Indians of all cuts to a lodge gave you two warriors. Hence, two warriors times fifty lodges came out Black Coyote. Maybe.

Nearing the village, a third thing began working in the back of his head. So far he had seen half-grown boys, squaws, small children, oldsters. Dart as it would through the camp streets and around the center square, his roving glance failed to bounce off a single full-feathered buck. From what a man could see, granting he was seeing wide and guessful, there wasn't a trail-grade warrior in the camp. One thing about that hunch: he could nail it down once he got into the camp.

That was a good guess, as far as it went. Trouble was, it didn't go far enough. A hundred yards out from the lodges,

29

three Indian horsemen broke from the nearest cluster of tipis. Riding abreast, the Arapaho bore down on Jesse, blocking his approach to the village. The mountain man reined Heyoka in, sat waiting, slack-shouldered and watchful.

The riders were old men, each of them clearly an elder chief and warrior of past reputation. Their spokesman, a withered giant wearing a red flannel undershirt, U.S. Infantry pants and a single scarlet heron plume slanting through his gray braids, pulled his pony up, facing Jesse.

"*Hau,* the white brother comes in peace?"

"*Hau,*" Jesse responded, gravely touching the fingertips of his left hand to his forehead. "*Woyuonihan!*"

It was the Sioux word and gesture of respect for the elder warrior of undoubted reputation. The old man was pleased but not, in this case, to be flattered off his original query.

"The *Wasicun* comes in peace?" he repeated, his rheumy eyes lingering on the beautifully engraved rifle resting across Heyoka's withers.

Jesse upended the gun, firing it into the air. "*Wolkota wa yaka cola!*" He intoned the phrase in the rumbling growl of the Minniconjou Sioux.

The three elders nodded seriously. *Waste,* good, this *Wasicun* talked with a red tongue.

The words Jesse had used were those engraved on the sacred ceremonial Pipe of Peace of the Sioux Nation. Their text and translation were known to every Plains Tribe west of the Mini Sosi. By their use the mountain man had pledged his real honor that he came without war in his heart.

"*Hohahe,*" the old man responded, using Sioux in courtesy, "welcome to our tipis. I am Old Horse. Here are Beaver Face and Spits-In-The-Wind."

Jesse threw a snap glance and a nod at the other two, swallowing the smile that wanted to follow the greeting. Man, you try and tie a redskin when it came to slapping the right tag on a package of goods. That Beaver Face had a set of filed buckteeth fit to make stovewood out of any six-foot sawlog. As for the Spits-In-The-Wind, the old devil's slack-jawed chin showed such a time-yellowed streambed of long-shag Burley juice that a man had to know, right off, he was as well named as his companion.

"*Ha ho,* thank you." Jesse made the courtesy sign, again. "I am Tokeya Sha, the Minniconjou. The Fox Lodge Brother of Ikuhansuka, Long Chin, and Mato Luta, Scarlet Bear." He threw the names at them, hawk-eyeing their graven faces for a wrinkle shift of recognition. Those were big names on the war shields of the North Plains and if the old coots were Black Coyote's boys, they'd likely know them.

But the old men sat still. They didn't share the flick of an eyelid muscle among them.

"Who is chief of your village? Whose village is behind you, there? Whose name do you serve?" Jesse barked the questions, peremptorily, like a Sioux chief talking to Mound Dwellers.

Old Horse was no Mound Dweller, and barked right back at him. "Heavy Otter. That's Young Heavy Otter, not the old man. And you will not talk to me in a voice like that again."

"*Wonunicun*, it was a mistake. Tell me, father," Jesse caught the old man's eye, pegging it down, "are you sure this Heavy Otter does not have a black skin? Big sharp ears? A bushy tail? You know, father. Much like those of a very dark-colored coyote?"

If the old man took the barb on that hook, he didn't break water over it. "My voice was clear. I said Heavy Otter. There is only one Young Heavy Otter. Him I serve. And no other."

"What does he look like, this Heavy Otter? I knew a Heavy Otter among your people when I was a boy." Jesse had never heard the name, was rebaiting his line for another cast at Old Horse.

"Short. Big belly. Weak chin. Bad color. Pale, most like a *Wasicun*." Old Horse eyed the mountain man, daring him to call the lie.

Jesse moved his shoulders, deprecatingly. "Let us go, my brothers," nodding toward the too-quiet village, "I would meet this Heavy Otter. He sounds like him I knew."

"No!" There wasn't any two ways about the tone in which Old Horse snapped that "no." It didn't mean anything but "nix." The Arapaho were turning their ponies with it.

"How do you mean that, father?" Jesse tried for a delayer, caught one.

The old man halted. "He's gone. Heavy Otter is gone. *Nohetto*."

"No!" The mountain man's own denial was as flat as Old Horse's had been. "That's not all!"

"Now what do *you* mean, nephew?" The first ripple of interest spread across the black pond of the old chief's face.

"The warriors are gone, too. All gone. Every one of them." The two gaunt oldsters backing Old Horse shifted their trade muskets to let them look at Jesse. Old Horse warned them with a scowl, turned to regard the white man. His leathered lips lifted, exposing the yellowed fangs beneath. Jesse imagined it was intended for a grin.

"Oh sure. You are right, nephew. Why should I deceive you who has lived among us? They're all gone. With Heavy Otter. Hunting buffalo. Trying to find some fat cows. Down there, someplace—" He pointed east, down the Black Fork. "That's why we are here. Just us old ones and the women and children, as you see. Waiting for the braves to find those young cows. That's how it is. Do you see it now?"

"Of course, uncle." Jesse knew the talk was over, carefully mimicked the old man's indifference. "That's how it is. I see it, now. Well, thank you." With the words, he was turning Heyoka for the emigrant camp, checked her suddenly, as though he had only been taken with a major idea. "Say. Listen to this. My manners are like an untaught dog's. Will my father not come to the *Wasicun* fires, tonight? Do me that honor, will you? There will be some roast mule, just the tenderloins and the backfat, and a few presents. A little *can hanpi,** maybe, uncle. Some tobacco, too, perhaps. Who can tell? My goddams come from the east at sundown, heavy loaded. Chouteau goddams, uncle. Big Company goddams. Carrying many things to the Blanket Chief at the fort. You savvy Big Throat? You see?"

"*Ha, ho,*" grunted Old Horse, delightedly. "We will come. All of us will come."

"Oh, no!" Jesse was quick. "Just those of reputation. Just you real warriors. Just you chiefs. Tokeya Sha feeds no squaws."

Flattered, Old Horse bobbed his head. "*Waste,* just the chiefs, then. We will come. When the nighthawk whistles."

Jesse saluted them as they rode away, turned Heyoka for the emigrant camp, his dark face scowling. Cuss their nighthawk whistles. He didn't like the looks of those old birds, nor of that big, empty camp they had come out of. The whole blasted river bottom was getting so thick with Indian smell it stunk clean to a man's moccasin tops. *Aii-eee,* brother. If Heavy Otter's other name wasn't Watonga, Jesse Callahan would chaw the core out of Andy Hobb's beaver hat!

---

*White juice of the wood, literally. Actually "white sugar," worth its weight in prime sable in any Indian trade.

Back at the emigrant camp, Jesse found Tom Yarbrough and three of the other men, Seth Mason, Brown and Hanks, waiting for him. There was no sign of Tim O'Mara and the others, nor of any of the women.

"Folks are resting back in the grove," offered Tom. "Tim's wandered off somewheres down the fork. Kids are with the women."

"It's all right for now," Jesse answered. "There's nothing to worry about from them Injuns right off. Their braves are all down the Black Fork running buffler."

The men nodded, apathetically, and Jesse continued. "But I want a guard stood just the same. The four of you keep your eyes peeled. If you see any mounted Injuns coming into that camp, or riding out of it, come running for me. I been riding all night and I'm tuckered. Right now I'm going back to the slough and wash off. Catch me a catnap, too, most likely. I been wide-eyed for near three days, now. Reckon it'll take me a couple hours to fresh up proper. Remember. Happen you see anything over yonder, fetch me instanter. You got that?"

More nods and a halfhearted assurance from Tom Yarbrough had to do for his answer. Heading into the grove and glancing back to see what the men were doing about his warning, he noted that Tom was talking to the others, apparently assigning them their guard posts. They in turn seemed to be arguing back. Jesse shrugged, turning his back on them. There was one stock of goods God never ran himself low on, and that was fools.

At the slough he shucked out of his buckskins and had his dip. The backwater was soft and soapy like all mountain water. It let a man's muscles down and lowered his eyelids.

Crawling out on the same bar where he'd surprised Lacey O'Mara, he donned his leggin's and stretched, bare belly down, on the drowsy sand. For two full hours he lay motionless in the deep, soundless sleep of the trained frontiersman, then came noiselessly awake. After an automatic moment of checking the late afternoon sounds of the prairie at normal rest, he relaxed and lay back once more. Half awake, half drifted off, his mind moved haltingly over the past crazy three weeks of his life. First off, there he'd been stopping over at Fort Bridger on his way to the California strike. Him and Gabe had chewed plenty of backfat over that idea, too, with old Big Throat doing his level best to steer him around it.

Jim was the first and the last of the old mountain men and he hated like tarnal sin to see his breed scattering away from the beaver streams and sable sets to go to panning for color in California or to whacking a string of bulls on the Santa Fe freight run. But, cuss it, the beaver were plumb cleaned out and the big outfits like American Fur and Chouteau & Company weren't paying fit enough prices, for even *prime* sable, to keep a man in shag-cut and bullet lead, let alone make any kind of a decent stake. If a man aimed to eat boiled dog and squat to squaw fires the rest of his mortal life, he might make some sense out of hanging around up in the Three Forks country or in moving on up into Canada to linetrap for fox and marten for some Hudson's Bay factor. But happen he wanted to gather a real stake and settle down, he could either go to working the Oregon or Santa Fe roads, emigrant-guiding or freight-skinning, or he could light out across the Sierras to see what all the fuss around Sutter's Mill was about.

It had been right about then, with him mentioning the need of that stake, that Bridger had up and thrown him this wildeye yarn about old Brigham Young plotting to burn him out of Fort Bridger, and him needing a *real* man to amble down to Laramie and tote him out a load of black powder so's he could bust the ears off the old Saint and his hardtail Mormon Militia should they be tomfools enough to actually come at him.

Well, that stretch of the trail brought a man smack up to Watonga and his now-you-see-him, now-you-don't, white partner ... and to those Kansas farmers and that reed-graceful emigrant girl ... and that bullhead, bad-eyed husband of hers. ...

Wide awake or half dozed, Jesse had stretched out on enough sun-warmed prairie spots to know that sound when he heard it. And to act instanter. Happen you could make the same racket with a pint-size casaba gourd and a short dozen brook pebbles, like the Sioux kids were always using to scare each other half to death with, but right now Piute Slough was mighty low-stocked on Indian offspring and dried melon rattles.

That was a diamondback, mister, and a man better believe he wasn't just buzzing his tail to keep the flies away.

Jesse rolled carefully to one elbow, getting his eye-level above the clump of lupine blossoms cutting him off from the origin of the whirring vibrations. If there was one thing he'd never learned to like about the short grass country, the six-footer sidewinder was it. He'd seen enough snake-bit poor devils to bloat up and turn bottlefly-black and take maybe seven, eight, ten hours to spasm-out and strangle to last him a long piece. Happen he never saw another prairie rattler, it would—

The running thought broke in midstride as the mountain man's gaze topped the lupine cluster. The frost-blue eyes narrowed to slits, the half-drawn breath dying in the uptake of the halted movement.

Beyond the purple flower of the bush, facing to him, a carrot-topped, freckle-faced emigrant boy of about seven was soberly stick-poking an eight-foot grandaddy diamondback.

The buzzing reptile, thick as a man's bunched bicep through its swollen middle, was just finishing its complete coil, the flat, triangular head, gaping mouth split clear past the ear pits, just arching back for the strike. Even as Jesse watched, the sickly, white swell of the puffed gum ridges was erecting the inch-and-a-half backcurve of the hollowed fangs and the boy, leaning forward in his absorption, had his unprotected face not three feet from the forking flick of the dancing tongue. Putting the prairie rule of one-third the snake's total length for the outside reach of his coiled strike to the present position of the youngster, Jesse knew the emigrant boy was a solid foot *inside* the boundary of certain-sure fang puncture.

There was maybe two seconds left. And if either the boy or the snake were startled—should catch any least movement of Jesse's before—

The mountain man's long body flashed forward, clearing the lupines as the reptile struck. His hurtling shoulder hit the boy two feet ahead of the blurred thrust of the wedged head, knocking the youth a dozen feet and banging himself jarringly into the big drift log where first he'd seen Lacey O'Mara. Before either the boy or the snake could have comprehended the six-foot bolt from the lupine bushes, the gaunt trapper had rolled to his feet, seized his long-barreled rifle and returned to the sand pit. Seconds later, silent-cursing and white-faced, he was splintering the diamondback's spine with the steelheeled butt of the Hawken.

Presently, his fury subsiding with the writhings of the smashed pulp that had been the rattlesnake, Jesse left off his labor of hate to turn to the big-eyed emigrant boy.

Picking the youngster up with one hand, the mountain man dusted him off much as he might have a piece of choice humpmeat which had fallen into the fire and gathered a coating of wood ash. Repairing to the down log he deposited the boy, seated himself, and entered into exploratory peace talk.

"What's your name, young un?"

For answer, the youth slipped the log and was off through the brush. Jesse dove after him, scooped him up, legged it back to the log. "We'll try it again," he nodded, pleasantly. "What do they call you?"

"You ain't the boss of me!" The boy's claim, neither defiant nor surly, was just plain statement. Jesse liked the way the kid said it and he liked the way he looked at a man while he was saying it.

"I ain't the boss of nobody," grinned the mountain man. "I *work* for my living."

"You do?" Apparently the boy hadn't known anyone in this category. His intense, round blue eyes ceased searching for a way off the log and started going over Jesse's powerful body. "Gee, you really got the muscles, ain't you, mister,"

"Name's Jesse, boy," grinned the youth's companion. "I don't cotton to 'mister.' Makes it sound like you didn't take to a man."

The big-eyed sprout was not to be so lightly swung from the principal attraction of the moment. "What kind of *work* do you do, mister? My golly, I ain't never seed so many muscles!"

"You ain't seed much, then, young un." Jesse was displaying no false modesty, many of the men in his profession possessing frames of a heft would shame a boar grizzly. "I'm a mountain man. What do *you* do?"

"Huh!" the youngster's snort was as wide open as his admiring gaze. "You ain't no such thing. Mountain men wear buckskin shirts with fringes all on the arms and things."

"I allow they do," agreed Jesse, stepping over the log and bringing his Sioux hunting shirt to view. The boy watched him, breathlessly, as he hauled on the shirt and toed on the beaded moccasins. Eyeing the youth, he asked, "Now then, what do you say, Red?"

"Where's your gun? And your hunting knife?" The skepticism, still on its feet, was wobbling badly.

"You seen me use the Holy Iron," averred Jesse, pointing

to the rifle where he had crotched it in a convenient cotton-wood after pulping the rattler, "and here's the knife!"

With the latter phrase, he whipped the Green River skinning blade out from under the buckskin shirt in a lightning belly-draw Waniyetula had bequeathed him, whirled and threw it with an underhanded wrist-flip nobody had given him. The razored steel drove into the log between the boy's spraddling legs, vibrated there like a tail-wounded copperhead. "What you say, boy?" the mountain man asked, quietly.

Mouth and eyes falling still farther open in the frankest of salutes, the redheaded youngster looked up at the narrow-eyed Jesse, and announced, admiringly. "I say you're a mountain man, sure as my name's Johnny O'Mara!"

"I might of knowed it," nodded the dark-faced mountain man, thoughtfully.

"Knowed what?" the youngster queried, puzzled.

"That you was Lacey O'Mara's son. You've got your mother's eyes, boy."

"Gosh, do you know my mother?"

"No, I just seen her in camp when I was talking with your folks back yonder," Jesse lied. "I don't recall seeing you, though, boy."

"Well, I seen you," grinned Johnny, "but I didn't think you was a *real* mountain man. Tim said you was a squawman and that you lived with the Injuns and liked them a heap better than you did your own white people. He said none of your kind was to be trusted on account you was red clean through to the middle once you'd lived with the Injuns. That's why I snuck after you when I seed you coming out here. I reckon most folks hates Injuns, but I love them. I mean to fight them and sneak after them and smoke the peace pipe and things like that."

"I allow every boy loves Injuns," said Jesse, soberly. "I know I sure do, and I was raised amongst them. Leastways, more or less, I was."

"Naw! You wasn't!" Johnny's denial was incredulous. It wasn't possible to imagine anybody being that lucky, to be raised up and to run around with real Indians.

"Heck, I wasn't," the mountain man countered. "The Sioux got me when I was a cub not much bigger'n you."

"Gee! How'd it happen, huh, Jesse?" Johnny O'Mara, as would have been any Eastern boy of like years, was purely

37

fascinated by the wild look of the long-haired, buckskinned figure beside him, and with the thought that here was a real, live white man who had lived with the hostiles and was still around to tell about it. The youngster's eager voice trailed off, disappointedly, as he failed to see his own excitement mirrored in the mountain man's quiet face. "Gosh, I reckon you wouldn't tell anybody about it. Not just a little kid, anyways."

"Shucks, boy," Jesse grinned, "not much to tell. I never had no mother, leastways not to remember, and the Sioux done my daddy in when they grabbed me—"

"Gee, that's terrible, Jesse. I—"

"Not so much, young un," his companion interrupted. "I reckon my old man wasn't against larruping me plumb raw, whenever he could take the time to get his nose out'n the jug to do it. Raising a boy up without no mother can be a tolerable problem, I allow. It sure was to my daddy at any rate. I allow I was fixing to run off, regardless, when the Sioux jumped our post and saved me the trouble. When you look at it long and short, I figure some growed-up men can give a kid more trouble than he can properly handle. I was coming twelve when them Hunkpapa killed my daddy. That's old enough to remember that I didn't shed no tears about it."

The mountain man's wide mouth had lost its ready smile during the brief running-back of memory's track, and when he'd finished, the boy beside him, taking his cue from the grim set of the dark jaw, was silent. But youth isn't constructed to hold a quiet very long when the topic on the table happens to be Indians. Shortly, Johnny gave in to his growing curiosity.

"Was them the Sioux what brung you up, Jesse? Them Hunkpapa? The ones that kilt your pap?"

"Nope, they wasn't, young un," the smile was back now, the rim-frost gone from the blue eyes. "I was a puny-looking squirt, sort of on your cut. And them Hunkpapa is great traders. They knowed a white boy was worth somewhat amongst the Injuns, more'n dang near anything, far as that goes. But their medicine man done looked me over and told them I wasn't going to make it through the winter. Said that come the new grass, that's the springtime, boy, I'd be done-in as a froze buffler calf. So them Hunkpapa up and traded me off to Long Chin's Dakota Minniconjou, and they was the ones brung me up. That's the whole gospel, Johnny. Them

Minniconjou took to me like they was my own folks, only a mortal lot better, you can lay."

"Gosh-all-hemlocks!"

"Sure. They give me an Injun name and everything."

"Honest Injun?"

"*Wowicake*, boy. Honest Injun."

"Was that your name?"

"Naw, naw. That means I'm telling the truth. Their name for me was Tokeya Sha."

"What's that mean? In American, I mean."

"The Red Fox."

"Gee! How come them to call you that?"

"Two reasons, boy," chuckled the mountain man. "First off, it was the red hair, see? That made the red part of it, easy. Then they hung the fox part onto that after I fooled them all by growing up. Old Long Chin, he said that any boy who could look as mangy and raunchy and slat-ribbed as I did, and could even manage to stay alive, let alone grow any must be smarter than The Sly Brother, that's the fox himself, boy. So they wound up giving me that name."

"Boy!"

"Well, I guess! Say, young un, how'd you like an Injun name? One you can be knowed by amongst us Sioux?"

"Shucks, I couldn't never have no Injun name. I don't even know any Injuns."

"Cripes, boy! You know me, and I'm the biggest redskin in the business."

"Golly, maybe you *could* give me a name, then. Just a little one, not too much. Nothing they'd ever miss."

"Why, cuss it, boy, we'll give you a real tongue twister. A chief's name. Regular Minniconjou too. None of your cussed tame Injuns. How's that?"

"Aw, you never would—" said Johnny, embarrassed by this windfall of good fortune, not yet ready to believe any emigrant boy like him could be as lucky as all this.

"Well, let's see—" Jesse deliberately ignored his small companion's doubts, "what'll it be? You want 'Little Dog'? or 'Short Calf'? or maybe 'Young White Pony'? Say, boy," the mountain man interrupted himself with a flash of his quick smile, "how about 'Red Eagle'? You know, after that red hair of yours, like the Minniconjou started my name. That's a real Sioux monicker, too."

"*Red Eagle*," the boy breathed the name like he was

39

tailing off a prayer. "Red Eagle, the Minniconjou. The brother of Tokeya Sha, the Red Fox. Oh, boy!"

"Ain't nothing to it," smiled Red Eagle's new brother. "Let's get a move on back to camp, partner. My wagons'll be rolling in pretty quick."

Tagging along, his freckled hand in Jesse's dangling paw, the boy kept quiet for twenty steps, finally found the courage to ask it.

"Say, Jesse, you know that Tim O'Mara? He savvies a lot about Injuns, too. Most as much as you do, I reckon."

"Yeah, boy," Jesse looked down at Johnny, suspiciously, wondering what tricky sidestream the spindly-legged tadpole was aiming to wiggle up, this time. "I figured maybe he did. What about him?"

"Well," the youngster's query shuffled the feet of its delivery a little uncertainly, "he said that when the Sioux Injuns give a name to a young warrior, they always give him a weapon to go along with it. He said it was a regular ceremony, called 'Canyon Kissy-cuppy.' Leastways, something like that. I ain't saying it's so, mind you. But that's what Tim O'Mara said."

Jesse studied the boy, narrowly, caught his wistful blue eyes wandering enviously to the soft tanned-leather thong upon which, hidden beneath the greasy buckskin shirtfront, dangled the mountain man's razor-edged skinning knife. His slow answer, not matching the quick twinkle in his lake-blue eyes, was a miracle of Sioux soberness. "Tim told you right, young un. The Sioux call that ceremony *Canounye Kicicupi.* That means 'The-Giving-Of-The-War-Weapons.' You reckon you're ready for a full-size weapon, boy?"

"Yes, sir!" Johnny's answer was prompt, his eyes still fastened, determinedly, on Jesse's shirtfront.

"I allow you are, at that," nodded the mountain man, easing the gleaming blade into view. "You know the Sioux most generally starts a young un off with a knife. Reckon you'd see your way to settling for this one? It's genuine Green River, boy."

The boy's hands were on the blade's shaft almost before Jesse could move to skin the thong free of his neck. Watching the youngster stow the weapon fumblingly inside his own hickory shirt, the mountain man took him by his thin shoulders, warned him with the gravest of mock seriousness.

"Now, listen here, Johnny—that blade's a Sioux Secret

40

'twixt you and me. See that you keep it hid inside your shirt, same as I did, and don't you never tell nobody about it. Nobody. Not ever. You got that?"

"Cross my heart, Jesse. I won't never tell nobody. I'll keep it so well hid not even a Injun could find it on me. Gosh—!"

Beyond a wide grin to show he was soaking up his full share of the sprout's enjoyment, Jesse Callahan paid the pledge and the return promise no more heed. Three days later, he was to know he had just made the biggest dicker of his entire life.

Andy Hobbs rolled the wagons in shortly before sundown, promptly put them in a tight box alongside the old fort ruins. Jesse pitched in with the parking, seeing no more of the newly christened Red Eagle, nor of his sleeky blonde mother. By twilight everything was snug.

Waiting for the coffee water to boil up, he had his talk with Chouteau & Company's wagonmaster.

After hearing of his brush with the three Indians and the vanishing white man, Andy Hobbs sucked noisily on his pipe, spat in the direction of the Arapaho camp. "What you make of them Arapaho lodges? Purty big bunch of them, I'd say."

"You'd be right." The mountain man's frown deepened. "Bigger than you think, likely."

"How big?"

"Black Coyote big."

"The hell!"

"The hell, yes—"

"How you figure?"

"Number of lodges comes out right."

"That ain't no real clincher. Anything else?"

"Yeah. No warriors with them. Nothing over there but squaws and kids and old people."

"You been over?"

"Halfway."

"They stop you?"

"Yeah. Wouldn't let me into the camp. Claimed it was Heavy Otter's village. Said the braves was all downstream running buffler. The big chief with them, naturally."

"Well, hell, it could be. That's sure as sin buffler country down there and this here's the time of year all the tribes is running their winter beef. Country's like as not crawling with Arapaho hunting parties from here to the Powder. I don't see how you're so certain this is Black Coyote's bunch, thinking of it thataway. Did you ask them about him?"

"Nope."

"How come not?"

"Wasn't ready. Saving that for tonight."

"We going over there?"

"They're coming over here."

"Why, dang it? You know I don't cotton to letting a big bunch like that prowl my wagon camp."

"I asked them. Wanted to give you a look at them. And maybe so throw a scare into this here emigrant outfit. The clodhopper fools want to head back down the Trail for Kansas. I'm aiming to talk them out'n it, one way or another. Going to try and get them to tag us into Gabe's and then wait for a strong outfit to roll east with. And don't get your back hair bristled about them redskins. I told them only the headmen and chiefs was to come. No squaws and no ragtag."

"What's the matter that this emigrant bunch is heading back?"

Jesse shugged. "Dead-broke. Food's near gone. Most of them old folks that ought never to have left Shawnee. Just like all the idjuts what starts for Californy with a brokedown string of played-out bulls and a slew of slat-bed wagons. Dammit, they ain't fit to crawl into the next county, let alone cover two thousand miles of cactus and riled up Injuns."

"Now hold on, Jesse. You been on or along this Medicine Road for better'n twenty years. You've seed a hundred and ten outfits like this one, and danged if I ever heard you offering to wet-suck none of them, before. What's chewing you, boy? You got yourself a gal spied out amongst them?"

"Not precisely, Andy, I just—"

"Listen, Jesse. I got a dozen wagons of bad-needed trade-stuff, not to mention that cussed Du Pont, to get into Gabe's ahead of the Mormon push. That's the way Chouteau writ the orders and by damn I ain't figuring to tote along no ragged-tail batch of splayfoot dirt farmers while I'm doing it. Besides, they've got the best idee of what to do, as it is. If they're short on grub and plumb stony, they'd best get on down the Trail for home."

"What about Black Coyote and that big Arapaho camp over yonder?"

"That don't mean a thing to me. We putten a crimp in Black Coyote's tail that'll keep his bottom tender for a

42

month. He's going to be too busy explaining how you beat him around Jackpine Slash to bother with any farmers like these here. Why, what in tarnal sin's he got to bother them about? The Crows done got their spare cattle already. There ain't a thing left to take off'n the poor buzzards. Look at them, boy! Cripes, even a Taos Pueblo wouldn't trouble to stop them to spit on. You mean to tell me a Big Medicine Injun of old Watonga's class is going to jump these here roupy Kansas jaybirds? Wake up, Jesse. Get back on the job Gabe hired you for!"

Jesse took the tongue-lacing and backed off. Hang it, the old man was right. Figuring it the way he talked, there wasn't a Mexican's chance in Texas that Black Coyote would bother the emigrants. The way Andy saw it made Jesse look like a pure ninny. But, brother Moses, the old coot hadn't seen Lacey O'Mara with her clothes off. Nor played with her gopher-faced kid, and made a Sioux chief out of him!

"I allow you're right, Andy. Guess having them Arapaho dogging our wagon ruts ever since Fort Laramie has got me smelling them where they don't stink."

"I reckon, boy. You just forget it. You go ahead and get to this purty gal and you'll feel better."

"There ain't no gal, you cussed old salttail!"

"Hoss feathers!" snapped the older man, turning to poke up the fire. When he looked back up, Jesse caught the quick drop in his voice. "Oh, oh! Shine up your Indian lingo, boy. Yonder comes your three friends. And then some, by God!"

Following the wagonmaster's gesture, Jesse made out a considerable line of Indians bearing down on the wagon corral, foremost among them the three old chiefs he had palavered with earlier. "Get them emigrants over here, Andy." The mountain man grunted the words, hurriedly. "And have Morgan wrangle that little red mule out'n the loose herd. That's the one what went lame on him back to the North Platte Crossing. Have him bring her up here. I promised them chiefs a mule roast."

The wagonmaster started to leave, paused, squinted hard at the incoming savages. Jesse, following the older man's gaze, narrowed his own eyes. The dancing yellow blotches of the cookfires carried out a hundred paces, splashing and dappling the approaching visitors with its shifting light. Behind the old chiefs rode a tall, extremely dark-visaged Indian. This rider sat stick-straight, naked legs dangling, body enveloped from shoulder to mid-thigh in a coal-black buffalo robe.

43

Even in the uncertain light, the hawk-feathered face showed savagely handsome.

"I dunno, Jesse." Andy Hobbs peered more intently before turning to go. "Maybe you're right. Happen they *are* bringing only the chiefs and headmen, like you told them. But, mister, if that big, mean-looking buck in the black robe ain't a squaw, I'll chaw crow till it runs out'n both my ears!"

4. PIUTE SLOUGH

JESSE fell flat on his scowling face in the powwow that followed with the visiting chiefs.

. . . Were they sure their tongues were straight? Did they call their real chief Heavy Otter with their hearts true when they said it? *Aii-eee! Their tongues were straight as war arrows. Straight as a Kangi Wicasi lance-haft. That straight. Not a shimmer in the grain of the shaftwood.*

. . . All right, then. The red-haired *Wasicun* had another name for them: Black Coyote. Had they heard that name! Watonga. Black Coyote? *Wagh! Had they heard that name? To be sure, to be sure. What Arapaho hadn't? A great raider, Watonga. One of the best. Woyuonihan, respect him. Respect Watonga. H'g'un! And say, had the Wasicun not heard that Black Coyote was down along the Medicine Road this season? Had he not met him along the Trail just now? Had the red-haired goddam guide not seen Watonga? He should have seen him, if his tongue was straight? If he was telling his red brothers the truth about having just brought those twelve goddams all the way from Fort Laramie. No? The Wasicun had not seen Black Coyote? Aii-eee! The red-haired one was lucky. The goddams were lucky. All the Arapaho knew Watonga had come south very early this summer. Wowicake, owatanla. It was a true thing.*

Andy Hobbs had looked across at Jesse, enjoying seeing the slick oldsters hamstring the big cub. These old chiefs were so plumb innocent and straight-out it made the mountain man look awkward as a six-hundred-pound cinnamon bear backing down a smoothbark sycamore.

The emigrants, too, bought the Arapaho yarn, whole-skein. After their bad-luck brush with the skulking Crows, these tall handsome Indians with their quiet dignity, impeccable manners and plausible intent to be the white man's best friends

45

struck the right note of assurance. Watching the nods and smiles of the gray-faced farmers, Jesse nearly puked.

The crazy, addlepated ostriches. You never took an Indian at his word. The minute you did, you had as good as given him a root-hold grip on your hair. And Andy Hobbs! By God, *he* had ought to know better. Yet, there he was, head-chucking the empty-grinning with the rest of them, like as if he'd spent the last twenty years plowing corn in Kentucky, in place of wading beaver streams and watching scalp dances. Even Morgan Bates, that aged-in-the-rawhide Trail rough, sat fat and stupid with his ears uncovered, enjoying the orations and handshakes of the Arapaho headmen as if this was his first trip up the Medicine Road!

Sneering at the whole business, Jesse wondered that ever a wagon got to Salt Lake, or a train to California.

An hour after the Indians rode in, they departed, leading Morgan Bate's little red mule and waved on their way by the good wishes of everybody in the white camp—with the notable exception of one very disgruntled and redheaded mountain man.

During the palaver, Jesse hadn't noticed the tall, black-robed "buck" Andy Hobbs had spotted for a squaw; had assumed she had been hunkered down in the shadows back of the outer rank of chiefs, where a squaw belonged. Now, carefully counting the Indians out of camp, after the prairie practice designed to prevent any red visitors being left behind to hide and spring a surprise attack, he missed the squaw again.

Well, probably nothing to that. She was undoubtedly the absent head chief's woman. That would explain how come she'd got to tag along in the first place. Now, she had evidently wandered off to poke and beg around the emigrant women while her menfolk palavered with the *Wasicun*.

Looking around the fire, he decided the skinners and farmers would squat around another hour swapping lies before turning in. Andy Hobbs was talking to Tim O'Mara and Tom Yarbrough. Morgan Bates was spinning a mile-high Missouri yarn for the remainder of the listening flathats.

Jesse eased away from the group without troubling to make a speech about it. One minute he was leaning against a wagon wheel listening with the best of them; the next, the wagon wheel was listening all alone. That strapping six-foot squaw was loose somewhere in camp, and Jesse meant to find where. Of course, while he was looking for her he would

46

keep his eyeballs skinned for any other squaws that might be wandering around loose. Like say, real light-colored ones. With maybe yellow hair. And for-sure blue eyes.

To make sure he got started proper on his search, putting the interests of the emigrant folk ahead of his own wagon crew, as was only noble and just (of course!), the mountain man headed for the little flicker of fires over among the Kansas wagons. Skirting the other vehicles, he drifted up on Tim O'Mara's old Pittsburgh, and paused back of a dwarf cottonwood about thirty feet out.

Tim had rigged a sort of flysheet of Osnaburg sheeting to make a shelter against the scalding suns and drenching dews of the upland prairies. This ran out from the wagon's tailgate. Under it, as Jesse moved in, crouched what he was looking for—both of it: the coffee-skinned Arapaho squaw, the creamy, gold-haired Lacey O'Mara. The mountain man had no more than begun to scowl his disappointment at so quickly finding what he'd told himself he was looking for, than he had something really unexpected to fret about.

Between the two women, laid down on a bundle of mangy cowhides, was a small child. At first, in the weaving firelight, Jesse thought it was the boy, Johnny, but as his eyes adjusted to the dark, he could see this kid had long curls. It was for sure a girl and a white kid, and it must be Lacey's!

Cripes. He hadn't figured on her having a whole setting of chicks. Just that smartpants little redhead cockerel, that was fine. But it kind of shook a man to think a girl as slick and slim as Lacey would have herself a whole batch of young ones. For the first time he began to wonder how old she was, and how long she'd been married to Tim. And how many other fuzzhead kids were stowed away under that rickety Pittsburgh.

While his mind wandered, disconsolately, his eye watched, professionally. And what it watched was the tall blackskin squaw. The Arapaho woman was making medicine signs and crooning some sort of an Elk dreamer song over the kid on the cowhides. When she went to prying the tike's mouth open and dumping some kind of powdered junk down it, Jesse figured he'd best make his walk-up.

He made it nice and quiet, like any Minniconjou. Neither of the women saw him until his sharp-growled "Hau!" startled them.

He didn't miss the flash of anger in the squaw's scowl, nor the unexpected brightness of Lacey's look. He kept his voice down, deliberately ignoring the Indian. "What's the matter, ma'am? The kid ailing?"

"Oh, hello, Mr. Callahan. Yes, the baby's sick."

"How long's she been thisaway, ma'am?"

"A long time." Lacey's voice sounded dull, hopeless. "It's the main reason I came out with Tim. The doctor in Kansas City said she ought to be where it's high and dry."

The mountain man looked at the wasted cheeks, pasty color, the flush spots over the tiny cheekbones. One look was plenty. The kid had lung fever. She was a goner, sure.

"Yours?" he grunted softly, feeling dumb for asking it, wanting somehow to hear her say it wasn't. Knowing, of course, it was.

"Yes."

"God Almighty, she's a purty little thing. How old is she?"

"Three."

"Don't look it, poor little devil. What you call her?"

"Kathy."

Jesse scraped his feet, ran his tongue around the dryness inside his mouth. Man! The way the woman stared at a man was like she'd never seen a real buck before. Made the short hairs on the back of your spine go to standing on end. Fumblingly, he scratched around for a way to keep the talk going.

"I know your other kid, uh, one of them, anyways. Little carrot-top about five. Buck teeth like a cub gopher. Him and me, we—"

"Johnny's seven, Mr. Callahan. And there's no others, just him and Kathy. He told me about how you were the past president of the Sioux Nation and that you were so smart and mean that when the other Indians saw you coming they all ran screaming, 'Run for your lives, it's The Great Red Fox!' Really, Mr. Callahan—!"

"Shucks, that's nothing," Jesse's grin spread, ear to ear, interrupting her threatened reprimand, "you should have heard about the time I tangled tail feathers with Watonga, the King of the Arapahoes!"

The rawboned squaw bent further over the sick child. Eyetailing her a glance, Jesse caught the bounce of the fire's flicker in the lynx-bright eyes. Under cover of her pretended hovering over the child, the squaw was watching him like a wing-hung hawk.

"Yep, that was the time, ma'am." His voice hurried on, wanting to beat the question framing on Lacey's full lips.

"Just happened down the Medicine Road a ways. Not six days gone."

The squaw glued her eyes to the child, not letting herself grab any of Jesse's bait.

"Old Black Coyote, that's Watonga, ma'am, he set a trap for me. But Tokeya Sha, that's me, ma'am, I was a mite too fancy for him. Tokeya, he jumped up and ran around Watonga while he was a setting watching the trap. The shame of getting himself outfoxed thataway, like to kilt the old chief. Him and his best hundred braves. Last I seen of them, them braves was thinking about making me chief, and running old Black—"

"Mr. Callahan," the blonde girl's break-in showed she was through monkeying. "Tim will be along any minute. If you want something here, say so and be moving on. Tim will never forget your hitting him, believe me. You'd best not be around when he shows up. He'll—"

"He'll do nothing," purred the mountain man, blue eyes whacking into the emigrant girl like a thrown knife. "And I do want something here, Lacey O'Mara. I want you."

Lacey's mouth dropped as her eyes went big. Before she could start to sputter, Jesse cut her down. "Not like you're thinking, ma'am. I don't mean that. But I do want to tell you how I *do* mean it. I'm slow with talk but when it's in me to come out, I got to say it. And I got to say it to you, gal. Alone."

"You can't see me alone. Tim would kill both of us, sure. And I don't care what you mean and I don't want to hear what you've got to say. I don't want to see you, I can't see you. I don't want anything to do with you. Is that clear, Mr. Callahan? I've got more trouble than I can bear, now. I can't do anything about you. Oh, go away, Jesse! I—"

The use of his name slipped out, awkwardly, interrupting the rambling flow of her words.

To hear her say it put a hot push to spreading up Jesse's spine fit to choke his wind off. To have said it, caused Lacey to wallow, blushingly, in her own confusion.

Eyes dropped, she turned her head away, stood fist-clenched, uncertain, angry. The picture of her in the fireglow, flushed, excited, tight-strung, did nothing to dim the memory of that cat's grace and strength of beauty which had first hit the mountain man's eye alongside the cottonwood bathing pool.

"You'll see me, Lacey." His dark eyes trapped her nervous

blue ones, refusing to free them for an instant. "Make it as soon as you get the little un quiet, and that clabber-head, Tim, bedded down. I'll be down there on this end of the slough where I seed you this morning. I got to see you and say what's in me. I won't touch you, without you want it. You'll see me, won't you, gal?"

"Go away, please. I don't want to see you. I *can't* see you!"

"Meeting's breaking up, over yonder"—the mountain man's warning carried Lacey's eyes to the group by the distant freight corral fire—"I got to skeedaddle. I'll be where I said, down by the slough. And I'll be waiting for you, Lacey."

She didn't answer but Jesse didn't miss the way her white teeth bit into her lower lip, nor how the dark blood came into her face, thick and fast. A man could be wrong, and a good many had stood in the rain all night to find out they were, but Jesse didn't allow he would waste his time at the slough.

Come an hour from now, and happen Tim got himself off to sleep without making any fuss, him and that gold-haired girl would have their talk down there.

Jesse, leaning his broad back against the big cottonwood log, sucked absently at his stone pipe. The pipe had been out for ten minutes but a man's mind will run a backtrack as good on a cold pipe as it will on a hot one—providing that track's as warm as the one the mountain man's thoughts were on. And Jesse Callahan's mind was really running. A man could scout a trail just so far, then he had to sit down and tote up the sign he'd seen.

The sign Jesse had seen so far had been mostly *red*.

One way or another, he couldn't get Watonga out of his head. First off, he had figured that after the failure at Jackpine Slash, the Arapaho chief would give up and go home. That had been before he'd discovered Washakie's story about a white man being along with Watonga was true. When he had found the Arapaho did have a strange white man with them, he'd had to refigure that part of it. Even so, he hadn't been too worried until he'd run into this emigrant bunch with Lacey O'Mara among them and with the big Arapaho camp squatting herd on them. And with that bad case Tim O'Mara riding guide for them.

Right away he hadn't liked the looks of all that. Then,

when he'd found the village empty of warriors and just of a size to match up to Watonga's number of war-party bucks, he'd really started to sniff his backtracks to see where he'd missed a sign he shouldn't have.

And he knew full well he had, too. Or maybe better yet, he *was*.

For one thing there was something about Tim, beyond his being Lacey's man and a standout settlement tough, that fretted him considerably. For another, that strapping big squaw, with her rawboned build and bold-out approach, kept hitting a memory bell that wouldn't ring. For a third, his "Sioux blood" kept gingering him about leaving the emigrants to head on down the Medicine Road, east.

Just because that bat-blind Chouteau & Company bunch of red-necked Missouri muleheads had joshed and rough-joked him off his hunch didn't stop that hunch from working. You don't spend twenty-two years eating half-raw dog and smoking yourself over a buffalo-chip blaze without you build up some trace of what every *red* Indian is born with—a sixth-sense nose, touchy as a blistered heel, for impending disaster.

The mountain man came out of his thinking spell, head sharp-cocked. "That you, Lacey?" His soft question went to the willow brush across the sandbar from the log. "Lacey, you hear me?" he repeated, quickly.

He got his answer from a couple of tree frogs and the chorus of water peepers in the slough fringe grass.

Waiting five breaths, he eased off the log, went fox-stepping through the dark. There was nothing in the willows save the wisp of nightbreeze that should have been there. "Could have been the wind," he muttered, doubtfully. "Man gets edgy setting up for something like *her* to show."

The hour he had given her was gone. Not alone that hour but a grudging and nervous half of the next one. Now he had to admit she'd likely meant what she'd said. Either that or she hadn't been able to dodge Tim. Well, if that was the way it was going to be, he would have to brace himself to seeing her in the morning. That, or forget the whole thing. Which, all things considered, wouldn't be a far piece from a good idea.

But where was there anybody around to tell a man how he went about forgetting something like Lacey O'Mara? Something with a top-cream body like that, and eyes that went deeper into a man than a broadhead buffalo arrow?

51

She came out of the darkness as Jesse moved back out of the willow brush.

Standing there in the starlight, motionless at the edge of the black filigree of the trees, she didn't offer to move or speak. Not even the tree-dark or the pale starshine could hide the poised grace of that figure. When Jesse came up to her, she looked down and away, like as though she didn't want to see him.

"Hello, Lacey. I'm certain glad you came. I was beginning to think you wouldn't."

"I didn't aim to—" The voice was strained. "Please don't talk yet. I—"

The mountain man took her arm, feeling the way it went tense under his fingers. "Come on over here, Lacey. We can set on that old log. Don't be feared, gal. Ain't no call to be, I allow." With the words, his hand tightened on her arm, urging her gently.

She pulled away from him at once, and he let her go, sensing the bowstring tautness running through her, knowing that the wrong word or move could set her off for good. "Come on," he repeated easily, turning to lead the way, not looking to see if she followed, "ain't going to harm us none to talk."

At the log, he turned to find her at his elbow. "Set down, ma'am." He made the words sound as calm as they could, coming from a man that was as tendon-loose as a bull elk with sixteen half-starved wolves ringing him in. "I'll give it to you, straight out."

She sank to the warm sand beside the log, saying nothing, still not letting herself look at him. Jesse followed her down, careful that he left plenty of sand between them.

"It'll save time if we don't whale around the brush, none," he began, nervously. "I never been in love with a gal in my life, Lacey. Now, I reckon I am. I want you to come on to Californy with me—"

"Jesse!"

"Don't break in on me!" The mountain man's order was rough. "I got it all in mind what I want to say. All I ask is that you set still and give it a listen. After that, you can have your own whack at it. How about it, gal!"

"All right—" The answer was so low, it took a Minnicon-jou ear to hear it. But it came without hesitation, and Jesse marked that.

"We'll take the kids and go. Now. Tonight. You don't take

nothing but them. Last I seed of Tim, he was killing a gallon of jug with Andy Hobbs. I reckon the way he's asleep now, a mule could stand hipshot atop him without Tim missing a snore."

He paused, side eyeing her before hurrying on. "That little gal of yours has got the lung fever. I seen it too many times in Injun kids to miss calling it. Best chance she's got is to get where it's mile-high and skin-dry. Your own doctor told you that and, by damn, Californy is full of places to fit that prescription. As for Johnny, he's cut to size for my kind of cub. Coming to you, Lacey, God help me, I can't tell you how it is. It's got me so strong I can taste it. I want to go on tasting it from here till the lantern goes out. That's all, gal. I can't say it no better."

The silence that mushroomed up was that thick Jesse thought he'd strangle on it. Still, when she spoke, the halting, soft way of it let him know he hadn't read her eyes wrong.

"You don't have to say it any better, Jesse. You've said it beautiful. I've never been in love either, Jesse. I don't even know that I am now. I only know how it feels when you look at me and how it squeezes here inside when I look at you. I've never felt it that way, before. But, Jesse, the whole thing's crazy. All of it. If it wasn't for Kathy, I might see it, might go with you, I—"

"What about Kathy?" Jesse interrupted, harshly. "What's she got to do with it, Lacey?"

"She's got to get back to a doctor, Jesse. I'm afraid Kathy's going to die! But I've got to get her there. Give her a chance. She's *got* to have that chance, Jesse"—the girl's voice trailed off, helplessly, her words as dead as the hope within them—"and I guess you know where the nearest doctor is."

"Yeah. The Army surgeon at Fort Laramie," he tried to give it to her softly, "and she'll never make it. That baby's going to die, Lacey. I allow you that."

"Jesse! Kathy's got to have a doctor—!"

The mountain man said nothing, knowing that where a mother's got a dying child she's rightfully got her mind flowed-over for anything else. After a long minute he asked the question which had been on his mind from the moment she had told him she was *Mrs.* O'Mara.

"How about Tim and you, Lacey gal?"

The emigrant woman hesitated with her reply. When it came, it was low-voiced with awkwardness. "Tim near hates me, I guess. I've not given him the kind of love a man has a right to expect from his woman. That bitters a man like nothing else—" The girl paused, her voice dropping lower still. "Tim's not the children's father, Jesse. I married Tim only to get Kathy out here. Their real father, my first husband, died three years ago in the settlements. Scraping around back there to feed the children those three years, with the baby sick and all—" Another pause to let the embarrassment creep thick and heavy into the emigrant woman's voice, and she concluded, haltingly. "Oh, I'm so ashamed, Jesse!"

The mountain man said nothing, waiting for her to continue. After a moment she did. "Well, when Tim told me he was taking this train as far west as Salt Lake and offered to take me along if I'd marry him, I just shut my eyes and said yes.

"Tim's a Mormon, you know, and I thought he would at least be good to us. But oh, Jesse, it's just been awful! The whole shameful thing of it. So when he refused to guide these folks back, I stayed with them to get Kathy back to the doctor like I told you.

"That's the whole story, Jesse. Of course, I never loved Tim and now that he's back, I'm terrified of him. Jesse, he's up to something, I know he is. I can feel it, and I'm scared to death—!"

The mountain man waited while his hand-galloping thoughts raced to catch up with the half relief, half alarm created by the girl's astonishing outburst. At the moment, he was too concerned with Lacey's and his own emotions to sort out the peculiar significance in her remarks about Tim O'Mara. And when his question came, it was deliberately and carefully off-trail.

"How old are you, Lacey?"

Her laugh was low, but not so low it hid the hardness in it. "Thirty-one, Jesse. Most thirty-two."

He had asked her only to change the subject, hadn't expected that heavy an answer. "God Almighty, honey, a body'd never guess it. You look eighteen."

"I don't feel eighteen, Jesse, and that's another thing." The bitterness was gone, now, in its place a sort of dull acceptance. "You look thirty and probably aren't a day over twenty-five. That's a lot of difference when it's on the woman's side."

He started to tell her he was full thirty-three, trapped the admission with a snap of his white teeth, sealed it with one of his quick grins. "Hell, Lacey, I not alone look thirty, I feel fifty. I been night-sleeping the prairie by my lonesome for so long it feels like I been waiting for a woman the past twenty years. Lacey, I reckon it ain't going to save you if you're forty. I aimed to make a stake out'n this trip and I got that stake more'n made, honey. I'll clear a thousand dollars on the peltries I brought down from Three Forks, alone. Then I got a five-hundred-dollar bonus coming for getting some gunpowder through to Jim Bridger up to the fort. Cripes, we'll have more money than ticks on a sick elk!"

She kept quiet a long time, then. Finally, her words were thought out, careful. "I've had a bad life, Jesse. I guess, you can tell that. I've not had a man the real way. I feel I could have you that way, Jesse, and I want to think we'd find the best kind of love together. But the way it is, I just can't quite dare myself into believing it. Jesse, I just *can't!*"

After a moment, she went on. "I don't know anything we can do, either. My folks have got to travel on, tomorrow. Your train has got to keep going to Fort Bridger. We're just moving in opposite directions, Jesse—"

"Lacey, will you leave Tim if I come back to Laramie for you?"

"Jesse! *Please* don't talk to me like that!" The sudden fierceness shooting her words narrowed the mountain man's eyes, put the blood, thick and hammering, into his throat.

His great hands took her arms, high up, burrowing their hard talons into the warm hollows of her armpits; his mouth, wide and cruel as any Sioux's, smashing her soft lips apart, writhing and thirsting for the sweetness of them.

She threw her head, fiercely, breaking the bruising kiss, surging back from him. Instantly his arms were behind her, trapping her against him, crushingly, demandingly. She came to him, then, soft-crying her throaty eagerness, her parting lips finding his, her round arms circling his cording neck, the drive of her body coming willingly to meet his, frantically hungry for a thing it had never known.

The lumpy three-quarter moon, loppy and tired as a canteloupe that has lain too long on the vine, took a polite yawn and went sliding into the hills across the Black Fork. The peepers in the fringe grass lowered their racking song to a drowsy hum. Somewhere down the slough, a plover raised his plaintive nightsong. Out-prairie, beyond the river, a sage hen muttered sleepily.

In the creeping shadow of the cottonwood log, other voices paced the slowing rhythm of the prairie night.

"Getting late, Lacey honey."

"Yes, I know—"

"I allow we'd best be moving back."

"Yes—"

Jesse rolled up on one elbow, lay there looking down on her, the last wanness of the dropping moon dappling them with its pale glow.

Lacey lay quietly, one arm thrown across her eyes, the other slipping around the monutain man's bare shoulder. Her fingers moved over the carved sinews, lingered wonderingly along the swelling curve of his bicep. There was no heat in the fingers now, no frantic urgency. Their slow coolness felt like nothing Jesse had ever had on him. He came into their touch, easing his body back down until it lay again against Lacey's.

The freshness and fragrance of her washed over him once more, but now long and lazy, like lowering your body into mossy springwater. He pillowed his head in the crook of her arm, pressing his dark chest gratefully into the moving swell of her cool breast.

"Lacey—"

"Yes, Jesse."

"You remember all we said?"

"I remember—"

The peepers took over, filling the little silence. "We'll leave it that way, honey. Like we last said."

"Yes, Jesse."

"You'll go on with Tim and your folks, back to Laramie. I allow you'll make it without no trouble with the Injuns. And I'll be back for you real sudden. We'll all of us, the kids and you and me strike out for Californy. You'd like that, wouldn't you, Lacey? Taking up where your folks left off, going out to the Californy coast?"

"Yes, oh yes, I would, Jesse. And I'll go with you!"

"Sure, honey. We know how we feel, now. That's the biggest part of it."

"It's the whole part, Jesse. You're the only man I've ever loved like this. I want that, Jesse. I want it for the rest of my life."

"Me too, Lacey gal." He rolled back with the tense whisper, letting her come in to him, his hands sliding down her arching back.

"Hold me, darling! Once more, Jesse. Once more. Just this minute, Jesse . . ."

"You're held, Lacey!" the wide mouth sought under the yellow hair, finding the lobe of the small ear, the muttered phrase coming with the kiss—longdrawn, fierce, relentless.

The stream of Lacey O'Mara's mind had tumbled in a millrace of confusion from the moment she had looked up to meet Jesse's level stare across Piute Slough.

From the first of the dry tears canonizing the crude couch of the settlement wedding night, her life had dropped into that half-dead hell to which so many frontier women found themselves delivered twenty-four hours after some circuit-riding God-talker had hustled through the holy words to drop the Good Book and run for the whiskey barrel.

Looking up to see the red-haired mountain man and the smoke-gray Sioux mare across the prairie bathing pool, the picture innermost in any love-cheated woman's mind had slotted into its golden frame—just as true and clear as ever that of any olden captive and despairing princess in storied ivory tower.

That rattailed, mud-dirty mare, with her popped eyes, rack-of-bones ribbing and hipshot stance, was the milkiest of white steeds. And most certainly that split-oak post of a rider, lantern jaw, lank hair, grimy Sioux moccasins and all, was the knightliest of armored errants.

Now, gliding toward the cherry glow of the wagon fire, her heart high with the excitement of the promise she had just concluded with Jesse, Lacey was suddenly terrified. The crouching figure hovering near the fire, its shadow bulking, man-big, against the rough boards of the wagon's tailgate, shoulder-shot her running dreams dead center.

Tim! God in Heaven! Somehow he had missed her, somehow been aroused from his sodden sleep, was hunkered there waiting for her. For a crazy moment she thought of turning back, finding Jesse, facing the whole thing out, here and now. A child's restless whimpering caught up the skirt of her impulse, sharpened her wide eyes.

The figure by the fire turned to reveal its craggy hawk's face, the small bundle clutched to its breast. The squaw! The big Arapaho squaw. Thank God. She was still there.

Lacey came to the fire, sinking down by the Indian woman, holding her finger to her lips, nodding toward the wagon-bed and the rising snores of its occupant. The tall squaw nodded back, with a quick smile held forth the figure of the sleeping Kathy, close wrapped in the pile of the black buffalo robe. "Baby much better. Baby good, now." The stilted words came in a grunt as deep as any brave's.

Lancey glanced at the child, noting the half-smile on the little face, the peaceful easy pace of her breathing. Dear God, she did look better. For the first time in weeks, Lacy O'Mara felt the sudden jump of mother hope. Her bright return smile to the Arapaho woman conveyed that hope.

"*Hau*," grunted the squaw, carefully shouldering out of the heavy robe, bundling the child in it, placing her gently by the fire. Under the robe, the squaw was garbed in a slip-over of tanned doeskin. From the breast of this she now drew a small doll, a strangely ugly thing, its warped features and small, twisted limbs fashioned entirely of dried buffalo hide. "*Hanpospu Hoksicala*," said the Indian woman. "Holy Doll, Sioux Medicine Doll. Very big medicine."

With the words, she placed the crude figurine in the robe with Kathy. The child turned in her sleep, smiled, snuggled the grotesque image in her thin arms. The squaw stared at the infant a moment, raised her narrow eyes to Lacey. "Me go now. Come back, soon. Come back with the light. With the sun."

"Oh, thank you," the emigrant woman's gratitude hurried out, "but you can't! I mean it won't do any good. You see, we're leaving in the morning. We're going to travel on. My wagons are going away then, you see? But I do thank you, uh—" The white girl paused, wanting to use the name of her new companion.

"Elk Woman. My name, Elk Woman." The squaw extended her hands across the fire, smiling. Lacey seized them, impulsively.

"God bless you, Elk Woman. I know my baby is better. Oh, thank you so much!" Her eyes falling on the buffalo-hide doll, Lacey added anxiously, "Can she keep the little doll, Elk Woman? See how she cuddles it, already."

"*Hau*," grunted the squaw, easing to her feet. "She keep. Me come back. Go now."

"But—" Lacey started to repeat her explanation of the emigrant departure, but the Indian woman held up both hands, palms out, asking for silence.

"Me come back with sun. Stay with baby. She get well."

"But, Elk Woman—" It was clear the Indian had failed to grasp the content of Lacey's straight-spoken English, did not

58

understand the camp was moving. "We are leaving. We go tomorrow. See? You can't stay with us."

"Me travel with you," the big squaw shrugged, simply. "Go get medicine leaves, now. Come back and travel with *Wasicun* goddams. Baby gets strong."

"You mean you'll stay with us? Travel along with the wagons? Nurse the baby?"

"*Hau*," the squaw nodded, vigorously. "My braves down river hunting buffalo. Maybe six, seven suns. Me go that far. Meet braves. Baby well, then."

"Oh! You'll stay with us till we meet your warriors. They're hunting down the Trail. *Hau?*" The white woman used her first Indian word with awkward hopefulness.

"*Hau! Hau!*"

"It would be wonderful! How can I ever thank you, Elk Woman?" Lacey's eyes were shining, her face high-flushed with color. When a person's luck turned, it seemed to turn all at once. Surely Lacey O'Mara's had turned today, for the first time in three long years. And it had turned with the arrival of the lean, red-haired mountain man. And with the dramatic appearance of this tall, black-skinned Indian woman. God bless both of them!

"You no thank Elk Woman," answered the squaw. "Me love baby. All baby!"

With her statement, her sharp eyes shifted to the shadows near the back of the canvas tailgate shelter. Stepping past Lacey, she bent over the sleeping form of Johnny O'Mara. Lovingly, the Indian woman tucked the threadbare blankets around the youngster. When she had them just right, she placed her right hand on the boy's forehead, whispering, intently. "*Han mani wolkota, Ya Slo. Hdi-yotanka!*"

And with that, she was gone, fading into the outer darkness with all the noise of a cutthroat trout sliding out of a sundapple into deep water.

Lacey looked after her, smiling happily.

For the sake of that smile, it was the Lord's blessing the white girl was ignorant of the *Shacun* tongue. All Lacey understood was that Elk Woman loved all children, and had paused to say an Indian blessing over little Johnny.

Well, maybe it was a sort of blessing at that.

Johnny O'Mara had a cheery whistle, practised its art more or less constantly. With true Indian direction Elk Woman had taken the habit and made a name for the *Wasicun* boy. She had used this name in muttering what Lacey so trustingly imagined to be her parting blessing to him.

Could Jesse Calahan have heard it, every hair on his red head would have rattled in its root socket.

"*Han mani wolkota, Ya Slo. Hdi-yotanka!*"

"Walk in the night with peace, Little Whistler. Soon you are going away with me!"

Jesse got back to the Chouteau & Company wagons about 1:00 a.m., rolled into his blankets, slept like a shot soldier until 4:00.

Rousing at that hour, he padded through the dark toward the looming shadow of the lead wagon. He waited a second, adjusting his eyes to the gloom, bent quickly over the wagon-master's huddled form, touched the tight-wrapped blankets, lightly.

"Andy—it's me, Jesse!"

The old man came scrambling awake, fumbling sleepily in the blackness for his rifle. The mountain man put a bony knee in his belly, pinning him back on his blankets.

"Hold on, you old catamount! I told you it was me."

"It's you, who? *Who* in blazes is it? Dammit, what's going on around here?"

"Shut up! It's Jesse. What in tunket's the matter with you?"

"The matter with *me*, you chucklehead? Don't you know better at your age than to go around grabbing a man out'n his sound sleep in Injun country? I mighten of shot your leggin's off!"

"You mighten," allowed the mountain man, "happen I hadn't of taken your gun out from under you before I shook you up. Leave off your grousing for a shake and pay attention. We're rolling out'n here."

"You crazy, boy? What hour be it?"

"Four."

"What's the idee? You know I never holler 'catch up' before five-thirty."

"I want to be moving before broad light. That'll be maybe an hour. There'll be light enough to catch up by in fifteen, twenty minutes."

"I asked you, what's the idee?"

"Hang it, you got a contract for hauling gunpowder and supplies to Fort Bridger. And I get a bonus for seeing that you do it without losing any of it. We're back of time on account of that mangy Black Coyote and his sneaky deal with Brigham Young. I'm thinking we'll have to roll soon's there's light to see, and to keep rolling far and fast from here on in. That is, providing we don't aim to let Watonga get set for us, again."

Up to this point, the mountain man had been making a very good case for himself, almost convincing Andy Hobbs he meant every word of his tirade. But as usual when things are going too easy toward a man, Jesse over-reached himself. Clearing his throat self-righteously, he delivered what was designed as the *coup de grâce*.

"But, mostly, Andy old salt, I'm wanting to get out'n here before them hangdog emigrants come awake. I'm feared they might change-up their minds and decide to tag onto us. And it's like you said yourself. We just ain't got no time to mess with them. Come on, rustle your tail, old hoss. Roust the boys out!"

The white-bearded wagonmaster cleared his own throat in turn. Spat contemptuously. "It's like I said, all right, young un. But you ain't quite quoting the part of it I'm thinking about. If ever I heard a young stud whickering over a bellyful of sour oats, it's you."

"What in thunder you mean, you mossy-horn old steer?"

"I mean it's sandbottom-clear that you tooken your try at that flossy gal you had sighted amongst them emigrants. It's just as clear that you missed it clean. Now, you're huffy about it and you're getting plumb away before you have to face up to her in the daylight, or maybe even her old man. Sure funny how a man will get hisself all bothered about something till she turns him down. Minute she does, he lets on like she looked worse than a clabbered cheesebag to him the whole time. You know what I think, boy? Hoss feathers, that's what!"

"We going to roll early or ain't we?" Jesse put the question sullenly, ignoring the oldster's center shot.

"Five's earlier than I like, let alone four. I'll split the difference with you, Jesse. We'll roll at five."

"Thanks for nothing," muttered the mountain man. "I'll see you at ten of."

"Going somewhere meantime, young un?"

"Reckon I'll sneak over and eye them Arapaho. Make sure they ain't moving out early too."

"Make sure they don't trap you at it, Dan'l Boone," cautioned the old man. "I don't hate you so purely that I'd want to find your thick head stuck in the Medicine Road on a sharp stake."

"I'll step soft," promised Jesse. "Just got me a four-bit hunch that something's stirring over there."

And, at that, there wasn't a thing in the world wrong with the mountain man's suspicion—save that it was a little more than somewhat late.

Long hours gone, Elk Woman had sent her hastily instructed messengers down the backtrail toward Wild Horse Bend and the waiting Watonga.

5. WILD HORSE BEND

RIDING the head of the wagon line, Jesse tried keeping his mind on the remaining road to Fort Bridger, and his eyes on the hills around it.

In the path of the lumbering Pittsburghs now lay the old familiar landmarks: Squaw Creek, Sioux Lick, Piute Butte, Black Timbers; fair enough places, all, to harbor a red-hued reception committee eager to readjust that little matter of the Jackpine Slash detour. Try as he would, however, the mountain man couldn't hold his thinking to what hostile possibilities might lie off the bows of his axle-squealing prairie schooners.

Time and again as the interminable morning wore away, his Indian hunch kept herding his thought back to the emigrant camp at Piute Crossing.

Cuss a man's mind, anyway. He still knew he had fumbled something back there. And it wasn't anything about Lacey or even about Tim O'Mara. It was something with those cussed Arapaho—most particularly that hawk-faced squaw. There had been something about her he should have tumbled to. Some one shifty thing that kept skipping around the back of his head and wouldn't stand still long enough for a man to get a 'membrous look at it.

An hour after noon halt, with the wagons rolling steadily over the hard-packed going and with him and Andy Hobbs outriding the lead Pittsburgh, the wagonmaster suddenly remembered something.

"Thunderation, Jesse! I just thunk of something. Here—" The old man dug inside his shirt, bringing forth a wadded scrap of yellow paper. "I was supposed to give you this. That emigrant boss's woman, the purty gal with the yellow hair, she brung it over while you were sneaking around that Arapaho camp this morning. I ain't read it."

Jesse took the paper, unfolding it and studying the enclosed writing, the frown ridges building up heavier by the second.

"What's the trouble, boy, bad news?"

"I dunno," answered Jesse sullenly.

"What the Sam Hill you mean, you dunno? You can read, cain't you? What's she say?"

"No," gruffed the mountain man, shortly.

"Well, boy, that's nothing. Lots of women have said no. Don't let them throw you. It's their favorite two-letter word."

The mountain man handed the paper back to Andy Hobbs. "I didn't mean she said no," he mumbled flushing. "I meant, No, I can't read."

"Oh," the old man took the paper, spreading it proudly on his saddle horn. "Well, that's nothing neither. I allow there ain't nobody in this here train what can, saving me. Let's see, here—

"Uh, 'Jesse, darling—'

"That's the way she begins it. Hmmm, now how does it go? Let's see, here—say!" The old man broke off, eyeing Jesse suspiciously. "Goldang you, did you see that gal, or didn't you? 'Jesse, darling'! Hmpfhh! You sneaky Sioux. And all the time here I was feeling sorry for you. Allowing you'd got your ears slapped back. Why, you ongrateful—"

"Read the letter, you nosy old goat. Never mind if I seen the gal or not."

Andy Hobbs, glancing at the mountain man, took due note of the way his blue eyes were darkening, and decided to read on with strict attention to Lacey O'Mara's ideas, foregoing his own thoughts with commendable good taste—and faultless good judgment.

Jesse, darling—

I wanted to see you to tell you that I'll be waiting for you at Fort Laramie. It's funny how everything seems to brighten up at once.

When I got back to the fire, that Indian was still there and she had made little Kathy much better. And then guess what, Jesse? She said she would travel with me and take care of the baby until my folks met with hers. Her tribesmen are buffalo-hunting somewhere down on the Black Fork.

Isn't that wonderful? I know that when you see us in Laramie, Kathy will be fine and strong.

I love you, Jesse darling. Remember me.

Lacey

P.S. Be careful of Tim when you come. He left camp early this morning after waking me up to tell me he knew all about you and me and that he was going to fix it so no white man would ever want me. He couldn't know about us and he has always been a bad talker. I'm afraid of him, Jesse, but I know I won't need to be once you're back with me.

The wagonmaster handed the crumpled note to the mountain man, along with a tentative grin. "Boy, I'm sorry I razzled you. You're fixing to marry that yellow-haired gal, ain't you?"

Jesse accepted the note and the apology. "Yeah, Andy, I allow I am. We're plumb in love and she ain't got no use for Tim O'Mara."

"Well, she's a looker," his companion nodded. "And that little boy of hers is cuter'n a fuzztail buffler calf. I allow you'll be right happy, providing you can work around that lunkhead Tim."

"He don't bother me no more'n a hobbled horse in a wagon corral," the mountain man muttered. "What gets my nanny is that slant-eye squaw. She's been bothering me right along, and now this tomfool gal of mine has to go and leave that red devil horn in and tag along with her and the kids. Hang it, for some reason, I can't help fretting about that squaw."

"Can't say as I blame you, young un. But I allow it's just the look of her that's got you riled. Man, she just plain looks bad. That six-foot build. Them wild eyes. That slit-ear mouth. Why, even the twisting way she limps around is enough to spook a tame steer!"

Andy Hobbs's rambling words sprung the trap of Jesse's reaching mind.

That cussed Arapaho squaw. The one that'd been hanging around Lacey. That one. He'd never seen her walking. Only riding in on her pony, then squatting to Lacey's fire. And now Andy had said she walked crooked! What was it his Sioux fosterfolk had used to call Black Coyote's wife? Wait a minute, wasn't it *Ousta?* Mister, that *was* it! Ousta. The Sioux name for One-Who-Limps. The Limper. *Aii-eee!*

He threw Heyoka on her haunches with a hackamore twist and nearly wrenched her head off at the withers. Wheeling on the advancing Pittsburghs, he dug his heels in. Going for the wagons, with the mare belly-flat, he stood in the stirrups, roaring like an arrowshot bear.

"Hold up! Hold up! Corral! Corral!"

By the time Andy Hobbs got his breath and kicked his old gelding to follow the mountain man, Jesse had the lead vehicles circling.

With the corral made, the red-haired trapper talked. And hard. The astonished skinners just sat their seat boxes and gaped. You couldn't even get your mouth half open, let alone spit a word out sideways of it, the wild-eyed mountain son was barking his orders that fast.

"Boys, we got us some tall riding to do. And, happen you like the sound of it, I reckon some high fighting. Get all this and get it straight. There ain't going to be no repeats." Caught up by the big-shouldered mountain man's intensity, the Missouri teamsters nodded mutely, none thinking to interrupt the hard gallop of words that followed.

"That big buck squaw which rode into our camp with them old chiefs last night was Watonga's wife. That village is Black Coyote's!"

Morgan Bates, as usual the first to put tongue to what went on in his head, drawled his challenge, tight-mouthed. 'Well, what of it, Jesse?"

"Just this!" Jesse jumped his answer. "Andy remembered something a minute ago. He handed me a note from that yellow-haired gal that was with them emigrants. That's the one with the little red-haired boy. That note said this here squaw, Black Coyote's wife, now, mind you, was traveling with the emigrants. She give the yellow-haired gal a yarn about tagging along to take care of her other little kid, the one that's puny, the little dark-haired gal. I allow you can all figure what's coming. Them red scuts will sandbag that bunch of farmers sure as we're standing here picking our noses. I allow the squaw is aiming to grab that redhead boy. Her and Watonga can't have no kids of their own. I remember that from hearing it camp-talked when I was amongst the Sioux. Watonga, he's dying to have a son. And, boys, that hard-faced squaw ain't against dying to give him one!"

"I reckon there'll be more dying than her," vouchsafed

Morgan Bates, "less'n we put a hump in our tails. How you aim to work it, Jesse?"

"Leave Andy and two men here with the wagons. You and me takes the other ten. Maybe so we can catch them emigrant folks before Black Coyote does. It ain't no secret I got more stake in that train than just saving them farmers. I'm saying that, right now, and asking any of you boys what don't want to go to sing out. Nobody ain't going to hold nothing against you, neither. You ain't getting paid for shooting coyotes."

"Man, I'm tired of mule-skinning." Morgan Bates's careless shrug picked up a following of quick grins around the listening circle. "Happen we can peel a coyote for variety, I'm for it."

"Let's ride," snapped another of the Missouri hardcases. "We ain't catching no emigrant wagons standing here."

The saddle herd was run in, each man making his own hurried catch-up. Twenty minutes after Andy Hobbs had mentioned the Arapaho squaw's limp, Jesse's coyote skinners were on their way.

Sitting the high-loping Heyoka in the midst of his little band, the mountain man nodded grimly.

A man had to be proud of his color, sometimes. There wouldn't be a man-jack of these boys worth his salt by settlement standards. They were every one of them ignorant as pigs and dirtier than a Ute's scalp. But where else would a man find another dozen such prairie-burnt buckoes ready to slap on a saddle and ride their bottoms raw for the questionable privilege of swapping shots with a hundred Arapaho hostiles?

The flat bowl of the Willow Bend of the Black Fork swam waveringly in the shimmer of the midafternoon heat mirage. Close to the river, as bone-stark dry as so many lunar craters, a glaring cluster of sandhills thrust up their bleached stumps to force the wandering wagon track inland and away from the stream. Beyond the hills, the sprawling half-loop of Wild Horse Bend threw the river once more back toward the Medicine Road. In the middle distance, crawling wearily along the desolate flanks of the sandstone outcropping, the inch-long string of dots that was the O'Mara emigrant train danced and wobbled in the blast of the dropping sun.

On the jolting seat of Tim's slatbed wagon, Lacey O'Mara clung to the blistering sideboards and fought down the rising waves of heat nausea. Behind her, in the canvas-shrouded oven of the wagonbed, crouched the fierce-eyed Arapaho squaw, her hawk-sharp gaze dividing its quick darts between the flushed child on the ragged cowskin and the empty sweep of the sandhills to the wagon's rear. Suddenly, the nervous glance steadied on the nearest, and last, of the silent sand-stone barriers. A white eye, staring as hard and long, would have seen nothing beyond the bulging swelter of the heat waves. But Ousta's was no white eye. And what it was seeing was no mirage.

With a grunt, the dark squaw leaned over the fitfully dozing Kathy, sliding one huge hand beneath the sweat-sodden little back, wrapping the other firmly around the wasted tininess of the infant ankles. Pausing, the Arapaho giantess shot a last glance forward through the puckerhole slit of the wagon canvas. *H'g'un*, all was well out there—the simple fool of a yellow-haired squaw half-sick from the fine summer sun—the proud little figure of the red-haired man-child walking beside the lead oxen, straight and strong as any chief's son. *Waste*. Now was the time.

No more than half conscious under the relentless hammer of the sun, Lacey came awake with a wild start as the coppery arm shot through the puckerhole to seize her rough-ly by the shoulder. "You stop wagons, quick!" The Arapaho squaw's sudden growled order burst threateningly. "Baby, her sick. Maybe die. She need water, bad. Now!"

Nodding desperately, the emigrant woman leapt down from the seat and stumbled forward along the wagon line, her shouted repeating of the squaw's abrupt order bringing the strung-out train to a ragged halt. With peculiar alacrity and total carelessness about the caravan's exposed position in the open meadow, Tim left the wagons the way they were, spurring his dusty gelding back along the line in an easy canter.

By this time the squaw had disappeared back into the wagon and was now leaping down over the tailgate bearing the close-blanketed form of the ailing child. As Tim rode up she at once began to cry out that fresh, cool water must be brought from the river without delay. On Tim's barked orders, three of the emigrant men grabbed wooden buckets and ran for the stream on foot. The instant they left, Ousta slid up to the startled Johnny O'Mara, seized the boy in one great hand, hoisted him easily to the bare back of her wheel-tied saddle pony and whirled toward Lacey, her deep voice falling low and tense.

"Him bad for boy see sick child. Child die, maybe. Boy no see. You savvy? Me take him. Ride up there little ways—" With the words, the squaw gestured quickly toward the front of the train, then moved to hand the bundled form of the silent child to the emigrant woman.

Lacey, taking the blanketed baby from the Indian woman, nodded, thinking the squaw meant to divert Johnny's attention from the serious fact of his little sister's condition. Three seconds later, she looked up, horrified, to see the so-called Elk Woman riding like the wind toward the spur of low hills to the train's rear, Johnny kicking and yelling across the withers of her racing pony.

The next instant, to the dumbfounding of all, Tim swung his gelding around the wagon and helled him into a furious drive after the fleeing squaw. From his shouts and yells, it had to be assumed he was dashing off on an instant and brave attempt to head off the Arapaho woman before she could reach the sanctuary of the hills. Heartened by their leader's unexpected burst of loyalty, the other emigrant men now broke excitedly for the two mule-drawn rigs in the outfit, meaning to unhook the long-eared hybrids and leg-up to join O'Mara in the chase.

But even as they ran, stumblingly voicing their new-found admiration for Tim, Lacey's scream stopped them short, that scream, itself, being in turn overlaid and blotted out by one immeasurably more shrill and pulse-breaking.

For a long breath, the emigrant men stood and watched the bursting cloud of Arapaho warriors boil out of the sandhills—boil out of them and come yammering and wolf-yelping across the prairie flats toward the stalled wagons. Stood yet another breathheld second as Elk Woman and Johnny, followed by the hapless Tim, disappeared into the rolling belly of that cloud. Then, Tom Yarbrough, alone among them retaining his mind, grabbed the dazed Lacey and whirled on his fellows.

"Hit fer my two wagons, everybody! They're mule-drawed and maybe can get us to the river. Don't wait to grab nothin' but yer women and guns. I got plenty of powder and ball and if we can beat 'em to Jed and the boys and get down back of the shelfbank yonder, we can maybe stave 'em off fer a spell—!"

With his shouted orders, Yarbrough was legging it for his

wagons, yelling for Seth Mason to handle the number-two hitch and to follow him full out.

Speeded by the ground-shaking roll of four hundred pony hoofs pounding down on them, the terrified emigrants, Lacey, still clutching Kathy, among them, managed to board the two mule-drawn wagons and lash them into an eye-white run for the river before the swarming Arapaho could cut them off. On the wheel-jolting, axle-squealing dash, they scooped up Jed Brown and his two water-seeking companions, making it to the shelfbank a scant hundred yards ahead of the wildly yelling Arapaho.

With the white men back of the cutbank and their long rifles beginning to bark a lead-slug welcome, the hostiles split their charge and pulled back out of range, leaving three of their number lying quietly in the ruts of the fleeing wagons. Mute testimony to the efficacy of the old prairie prescription for Indian Fever—a half-ounce galena pill administered in the belly without benefit of the mouth.

Now began an interminable ten minutes during which the Arapaho proceeded to powwow the advisability of further assault. Black Coyote's towering figure, unmistakable under its sinister eight-foot warbonnet trademark, was plainly visible as he rode the front of the packed warrior ranks, exhorting them to return to the attack. Then, as the hostiles hesitated, an even more sinister figure moved out of their ranks to join Watonga in haranguing them to wipe out the rest of the white men. Not a member of the tense group under the cutbank failed to identify this latter figure, nor would any of them ever forget the sick feeling it gave them.

Beyond any reasonable doubt of distance or overwrought nerves, it was the hulking, bear-thick form of Tim O'Mara.

When Jesse's dust-bearded riders rounded Willow Bend of the Black Fork to gallop into cross meadow view of the mile-distant loop of Wild Horse Bend, the damage was already done.

Not that he hadn't known it would be, curse the red sneaks. Two miles back on the trail he'd seen the grease-black smoke of the burning wagons snaking skyward. Now, as he checked his eager handful of would-be rescuers, he got the whole picture.

Two wagons had somehow made it to the Fork, and from behind them and a convenient shelfbank of the river, the white survivors were standing the Arapaho off. The other
70

wagons, amid a shambles of dead and dying oxen, were burning freely in mid-meadow. The hostile horde was for the moment milling around about five hundred yards to the west of the emigrant barricade, apparently undecided and arguing as to the next move. Their position put them nearly as close to Jesse and his men as it did to the emigrants—a fact which was instantly due to make the mountain man regret his hasty break out into full meadow view of the hostiles. For where his hard blue eyes were quick to see and size up the situation, they were no quicker than Watonga's piercing black ones.

The giant chief broke off his warrior harangue in mid-guttural, his thick arms sweeping westward with his barking discovery cry to bear directly on Jesse and the halted teamsters. A hundred red throats took up his harsh warning-word, rolling out their verification of the chief's gesture with a wolf clamor that lifted every hair in the mountain man's little group clean off the sweating white scalp that held it. Before Jesse could so much as think of an order, much less shout one, fifty of the angry braves were quirting their pot-bellied ponies straight for him.

The white scout had time to see two things before his belated command got into shouted being: Watonga was staying with the half of the Arapaho remaining in mid-meadow; the leader of the yelping charge toward him and the Chouteau skinners was a *white* man!

"Hit back for that last hill we passed, Morgan!" His words went to the quiet boss skinner at his side. "We got one wet-weasel chance, happen we play it right!"

In response, the teamsters swung their lathered mounts westward, racing back toward the hill. Behind them the Indians, aroused by the unexpected retreat, compounded their war cries with delighted insults and shouts of derision. *H'g'un! H'g'un!* The white dogs were fleeing without firing a shot. The vaunted Red Fox of the Minniconjou was running like any rotten-hearted village cur!

As Jesse held Heyoka's flying gallop down to the labored pace of the company horses, his deep voice was cracking out a continuing string of field orders. "When we hit the hill, hold in close to the base. Follow it on around to where we passed that sharp-angle jut. Pull in behind that and hold up, hard. They won't see us till they make the turn themselves—"

Seconds later, the skinners whipped their mounts around the indicated sandstone spur and haunchslid them to a jaw-pulled stop. Jesse's voice, held low beneath the pursuing clamor of the hostiles, gave them the final grim instruction. "All right, boys, I'll drill the first son of you as fires his gun. When they hit into us, club your pieces and feed them the butt ends. We got one shot apiece and we ain't going to have time to reload short of the river."

"What you aiming to pull, Jesse, a bare-hand ride-through?" The tight query came from Morgan Bates.

"That's it, boys." The mountain man's voice had to rise, now, above the bend-near yelling of the Arapaho. "Don't nobody hold up for no personal wars. We ain't ready to kill Injuns just yet. I'll try and floor that white polecat, but the rest of you get on through and back out into the meadow. After that, we hit for the wagons, and there—don't none of us take no for a answer from nobody. You got that?"

"We got it," nodded Morgan Bates. "Yonder they come!"

"And yonder we go!" hissed Jesse, slamming his heels into the skittering Heyoka. "*Hii-yeee-hahhh!*"

The first intimation the Arapaho had that they'd underrated the condition of Tokeya Sha's heart was when the harsh-throated panther scream of the Minniconjou war shout broke on their startled ears. The next, was the rebel-yelling appearance of the inspired Chouteau skinners, bombarding their heavy company horses around the sandstone wall to slam them, shoulder-on, into the galloping Indian ponies.

The Sioux war cry was always bad enough medicine to the sensitive Arapaho ear, but in this case the wild-eyed, red-haired vision that came with it was too much. Jesse's layback surprise worked like a dried-navel war charm. The hostiles broke wide under the impact of the teamsters' charge—broke wide and closed too late. By the time the outwitted Arapaho got their bucking mounts under control, the skinners had won through them, were free of the hill and racing once more into the open meadow.

Tim, gray-faced with rage, climbed painfully back aboard his caught-up pony, jerked the hackamore rope from the warrior who held it, cursed the disorganized Indians into a wheel-about pursuit of the escaping skinners. That Sioux-bred, bandy-legged beaver trapper! That buckskin-bellied squawman! He'd get that son if it took him his last breath. It was bad enough getting suckered by the oldest dodge in the Plains Indian warbook, but to—on top of that—get knocked, belly sprawling, out of your cussed saddle by a lucky swipe of the red-haired buzzard's Hawken butt was more than a man

72

could gulp down. "*Hee-yahh! Hee-yahh! Onhey, Wasicun! Onhey!* Kill the White Devil! Don't let him get away!"

For its part, Jesse's mind was as full of Tim as was O'Mara's of the mountain man. But with fifty insulted Arapaho bucks pounding his flying tailpiece and fifty more between him and those white wagons, yonder, a man's mind had to make room for more than Tim O'Mara.

"Keep up, keep up!" The mountain man's plea was flung over his shoulder, as he fought to keep Heyoka down to the skinners' pace. "Don't bother about them buzzards behind us. Hang low on your hosses and hold your lead till yonder bunch hits us!"

The reference was to Watonga's fifty braves, now following their bellowing chief in a ragged rush toward the fleeing teamsters, and Jesse kept repeating it incessantly. "Hold your lead, boys. Hold your lead. Let them get in, belly close. Steady, now. Steady—"

"*Hee-yahh! Hee-yahh! Onhey, onhey!*" Watonga's roar was echoing Tim's now, his screaming followers not a hundred yards from the Chouteau skinners, those of the renegade emigrant guide not fifty behind them.

Indian lead was flying now, thick as hailstones in a blue-blizzard norther, and men were going down. But not white men. Jesse had figured the Indian weakness for excitement and bad markmanship, plumb center. The converging fire of the two Arapaho groups was whistling harmlessly over the heads of his saddle-bent skinners and was raising billy-hell in the Indian ranks themselves. Perforce, at the very moment the two hostile bands had the Chouteau teamsters between the jaws of the prairie nutcracker, they had to slack off their firing. It was the split second the mountain man had played and prayed for. His wild shout called it instantly, his own Hawken's burst signaling the skinner volley.

"Now, boys! In the belly! Hold low—!"

When ten rawhide roughs cut loose with mountain rifles at twenty-five yards into a straggling pack of crazy riding red men, there's bound to be tall wailing in the tipis for some time to come. The sodden whack of the teamsters' lead tore a twenty-foot hole in the yelling belly of Watonga's charge—a twenty-foot hole through which Jesse and his long-haired mule skinners drove their tired horses headlong, to come pounding out the far side with nothing between them and the emigrant barricade but four hundred yards of buffalo grass!

Tim and Watonga were still trying to untangle the pony-squealing, warrior-cursing melee cause by their respective forces riding head-on into each other, when Jesse and his men slid their windblown mounts over the shelfbank and down into the cheering white-river fortress. And the Arapaho had no more than just gotten their pitching ponies' heads back up from between their knees, when the first of the reloaded skinners' lead began arriving among them from the reinforced riverbank.

Aii-eee! Nohetto! It was enough. MORE THAN THAT. It was too much! *Hopo*, let's go. *Hookahey, hookahey!* Let's all get far away from here!

Suiting their action to the Indian word for it, the Arapaho *got!* And they didn't stop getting until they'd pulled their scrawny ponies a solid eight hundred yards away, to sit them in fist-shaking, insult-shouting anger, safe atop the crest of the ill-fated sandhills. A moment, only, they hesitated there, forming a harshly beautiful background of painted horses and tasseled lances for the frontispiece silhouette of Watonga's eight-foot warbonnet. Then they were gone—fading back into the bleached silence of the sandhills as suddenly and unheralded as they had come.

By the way the hostiles had broken and retreated rather than sticking around to make an all-out fight of it, Jesse knew, even before he turned to the staring-eyed emigrant survivors, that Watonga had already gotten what he'd come for—whatever that might prove to be.

And what it proved to be was his own certain-sure hunch—Lacey O'Mara's redheaded son, Johnny.

Moving now to the side of the crouching emigrant woman, he got the entire tragedy from her compressed lips, the recital coming with an icy, blank-look composure that narrowed the gaze of the listening mountain man. As she told it, Morgan Bates, on Jesse's cold grunted order, was putting his skinners to shooting the dozen wounded Arapaho through the heads, and to helping the emigrants bury their own two dead and tend their wounded.

The mountain man and the dry-eyed emigrant girl crouched against the shelfbank while Lacey told her story, Jesse not touching her or interrupting her, knowing the least sign from him might precipitate the breakdown he could see building behind her staring eyes.

All through the stumbling recitation, she clutched the huddled form of her daughter hard against her, not looking at

74

the child, not even seeming to know she held her. When she finished, she remained crouching against the caving sandbank, looking glassy-eyed right through the mountain man.

Jesse reached over then, taking the pitiful bundle from her. A glance at the egg-shell crush of the small face, blood-smeared and wide-eyed, showed him the squaw must have heel-swung the child's head against the inner sideboards of the wagonbed. He muttered to the stony-calm mother.

"She's dead, Lacey gal."

The emigrant woman did not appear to hear him and he touched her on the shoulder. "Lacey, I said she's dead. Kathy's done for, honey."

Lacey nodded, dully, her eyes contracting as her face muscles pulled her lips up into the blank smile. "Dead," was all she said, before starting to laugh.

Jesse dropped the child, leaped for her mother. Seizing her by the dress front, he swung his hand, hard and dry as a cedar chunk, across her mouth.

"Shut up, Lacey! Shut up!"

He shook her like a bear with a range colt in his jaws. The laugh kept coming. Harsh. High. Crazy.

Stepping back, Jesse sighted the writhing mouth, smashed one short right-hand jolt up under the slack chin. Lacey's head flipped back, dropped, sagging forward, the mountain man moving in and catching her as she fell. Easing her slumped form down beside that of the dead child, he legged it up the sandbank.

Minutes later, the shocked survivors of Watonga's raid were being loaded into the two mule wagons.

"We put the bodies in that water-cut over yonder." Morgan Bates pointed the shallow grave to Jesse. "We heaved some loose sand and rocks over them—enough to hold off the buffler wolves. Ain't much else we could do."

"How many dead?"

"Two. Jed Brown and his old woman. Any back of the riverbank where you was?"

"Just the little gal," Jesse answered.

"Well, that makes three, all told," nodded the boss skinner. "And there's two more ain't going to make it back to the fort. Arrow-shot, plumb bad. They're so full of feathers they'd fly if you launched them."

"All right, then," the mountain man nodded, "you're set to roll. You oughtn't to have no trouble making it back to the Company wagons."

"What you mean, *we* oughtn't? Ain't you coming?" Morgan Bates eyed Jesse, waiting with his fellow skinners for the mountain man's answer.

"Nope, reckon not. The sons grabbed that little redhead boy the same as I figured they would. I got a stake in that kid and I mean to look after it. And another thing, too"— Jesse paused while his blue eyes swept their faces—"I owe the pot a few dollars for not pegging Tim O'Mara, right off. He's the white son that's working for Brigham Young in this deal. Cripes, I been dumb as a Mexican mule. He's a Mormon, he ditched this train to go on up to Salt Lake, he shows up again right along with Watonga's village, he gets it from the squaw about me taking this woman away from him—man! The whole stinking mess is my fault, and boys, I aim to clean it up. Beginning with Johnny and ending with that Indian dealer, O'Mara!"

"Talk's cheap," Joplin Smith, one of the Missouri hardcases broke in acidly. "How you aim to get the kid back? Why, they probably knocked his brains out the minute they got him behind them hills."

"Joplin, I don't know how I'm going to do it," Jesse scowled. "But one thing I do know. They ain't harmed the kid, and they won't. Not short of us getting him away from them, they won't." The mountain man paused, regarding the silent men with his strange, quiet eyes before continuing.

"That big squaw is barren and she's set on getting a son for Watonga. Well, she's got him now. She sure ain't going to club him. I know how them hostiles are with boy kids. Happen they knock over a settler outfit they'll near always sculp the little gals and hoist the boys. They're locoed on boy kids. If they wasn't, I wouldn't be here to know about it. I was grabbed out'n a Injun burn-out like this one when I wasn't much more'n Johnny O'Mara's age. And I know what they'll do with that kid."

There was another eye-sweeping pause, then, and the mountain man concluded harshly. "The boy's mine now, and I ain't hankering to have no son of mine brung up Arapaho style."

"You're rocking your head-hobbles, Jesse," Morgan Bates shook his head stubbornly. "You can't get that kid away from them. If you manage to get close to doing it they'll kill him. Allowing they're the same about it as the Comanches and Kiowas down along the Sante Fe, they will."

"They ain't no different, Morgan. That's what's sweating me, too. Right off, I ain't got no ready answer for you, neither. But we, all of us, have got to do what we can."

"Such as what?" the dry-voiced Joplin Smith asked.

"Well," the mountain man's answer rapped out, unhesitatingly, "you boys get this emigrant bunch moving for our wagons. When you get there, tell Andy to hit for Gabe's fort, instanter. At the fort you can gather up some help and come along after me. Happen I can track Watonga till you get back with that help, maybe we can figure some way to snatch the kid."

"How the devil you expect us to find you?" the boss skinner's demand was short. "Even providing we can get a bunch together what's willing to try?"

"That ain't so hard as it might appear, right off. I figure them Arapaho to head north, pretty much following the main line of the Medicine Road for quite a spell. They're looking for buffler and when a northern Injun looks for buffler, he don't look no place quicker'n he does Cheyenne Mesa. That's over west of the main road, and the road's the cleanest trail to take to there from this part of the country."

"All right, Jesse. I reckon there ain't nothing else to do. But me, I wouldn't give all the powder you got in that red-wheeled Pittsburgh for your chances of getting that boy back, alive."

The mountain man, narrow eyes flashing, pounced triumphantly on the boss skinner's laconic statement. "By Tophet, Morgan, that's it! The *powder!*"

"Bridger's powder—?" The skinner's interruption showed his failure to follow the thought.

"Oh, of course I know the stuff ain't mine to trade," Jesse raced on, "but under the circumstances I allow Old Gabe'll give me the loan of half of it against that stack of peltries I brung down from the Three Forks. And, mister, Watonga would give his right arm clean up to the shoulder to get even *half* that high-grade Du Pont!"

"Holy smokes, Jesse!" the lank Joplin exploded admiringly. "You mean to swap the Injun the powder for the kid!"

"Why, sure. I don't see how in the Lord's good name we can miss! Happen you and Morgan and the boys can get them emigrants on up to Gabe's, pick up some help there and come along up the main trail with that Pittsburgh and a dozen kegs of that Du Pont, and do it all fast enough, we got that boy back sure as buffalo chips burn—!"

The mountain man broke his words, the blue eyes leaping to Morgan Bates with sudden intensity.

"Not forgetting, Morgan, that along with the gunpowder I want you should bring me a good stiff coil of 'touch-off medicine'—just in case!"

Breaking out his wolf grin, the lean boss skinner nodded his understanding of the final cryptic instruction, expressed his agreement with the general plan, reservedly. "There's a chance, all right. Allowing you can keep the trail without being caught at it, the Injuns follow the Medicine Road like you figure, you can open your dicker with them without they get jumpy and brain the kid, and that even with the powder you can get that red vixen to leave go of the boy—them and about forty other 'maybes' I can think of."

"We got to gobble them 'maybes.' What you say, boys? You all game for it?"

"I reckon," shrugged Joplin, unhesitatingly. The quick agreement was backed by a wave of sober nods from his fellow skinners, Morgan Bates putting the official Company signature on the hasty contract with his slow-drawled grin.

"Me, I ain't got nothing to lose but a few day's pay and a scalp that ain't been washed since last July. Besides, I ain't never felt right about us crooking poor Black Coyote out'n his honest deal with Brigham Young and his blessed little Saints. I dearly love them Mormon buzzards and anything I can do to prove it to them, I aim to get done. I got a daddy and two brothers was kilt in them Saintly riots around Nauvoo* back in 'forty-four, and I reckon they'd want me to make it up to old Brigham. Jesse, if you aim to finish delivery of that Du Pont to Watonga, I'll skin your red-wheeled wagon for you!"

"You'll get your pay," Jesse Callahan's blue eyes were snapping, "and hold on to your hair, too. And finishing delivery of that Du Pont is what I aim. After all, old Brigham's a white man no matter what you Christian gentiles think. And he's given his bounden word that Watonga's to get that powder. Out'n my own great love and respect for my red brothers, I got to see that the straight-give word of us whites ain't allowed to green-up with no tarnish!"

---

* Navoo, Illinois; the capital city and stronghold of Mormonism in the midwest from which they fled after the lynching of Joseph Smith in 1844.

Many a center shot is fired for a hard joke. Unknowingly, the wide-mouthed mountain man had got his slug of cynical lead square-in behind the left shoulder of immediately future fact.

He found the bullet hole a sight quicker than he was looking to.

6. CARSON'S CANYON

JESSE made no effort to follow Watonga's war ponies. Instead, he headed back for Piute Crossing.

He knew Ousta would have ordered the village to knock down the tipis and pull out as soon as the emigrants left, knew also that it was a mort easier to track a fifteen-hundred-head horse herd and a passel of old men and squaws than to stick to a hundred high-traveling trail raiders like Watonga's war party.

He was righter than rockets on the day after the third of July.

The village track lay north and west, just as it ought, to cut the Medicine Road like he'd figured. And it lay broad and clear as a bull's bottom in a Sharp's sight. A blind squaw could have followed it backward in a fog thicker than boiled dog soup.

Jesse Callahan was neither dim-sighted, nor did he wear a cradleboard. And the weather was clearer than a first-prize glass eye. He caught the village just as the long prairie twilight was playing out to pure black.

Next morning, he gave them an hour's start, then set off dogging them, keeping to the west and well back. He expected to have some company from the east soon, and wanted to give them ample room to move in peacefully. Watonga should swing out of the tumbled hills to the mountain man's right before very long, now, to make his join-up with the moving village. That is, he should if Jesse had things figured right.

He had.

Black Coyote's bunch, with Johnny, Tim and Ousta, cut into the village track ahead of Jesse, about 10:00 a.m., passing so close to the granite outcropping back of which Jesse and Heyoka were hiding that in spite of her severe training along such lines, the mountain man nearly had to strangle the little

Sioux mare to prevent her whickering a lethal welcome to the nose-close Indian ponies.

Jesse got a real, big-eye look at the whole flashy parade.

Watonga bigger and blacker than ever in the clean morning sun, rode first, impressively haloed by the eight-foot aura of his white eagle warbonnet, the gargoyle-faced Ousta jogging, hardeyed, at his side.

Between them, in a place of honor that would have dazzled any frontier boy of seven, and whistling free and easy as though he'd been delivered of an Arapaho squaw in the first place, Johnny O'Mara trotted proudly on a beautiful little calico pony.

Jesse couldn't help grinning at the cheeky little sprout, sitting there on that sawed-off paint, chipper as a jaybird in a berry bush. Either the kid was dumber than all get out, or he was smart enough to play it happy. Whichever way, it made no difference. What counted was that he was well and frisky and showing more spunk than a spit-face kitten.

Back of this honor group, cantered Black Coyote's High Command: Gray Bear, Elk Runner, Yellow Leg, Blood Face, Toad and the canine-jawed Dog Head—preciously remembered faces, all of them, to the tensely waiting Jesse.

Behind the subchiefs, atop a wheezing pack pony, came Tim O'Mara. And the way he came spread Jesse's blue eyes with justifiable surprise. Where the mountain man would have guessed the Indians would have been escorting the renegade Mormon like an honored guest, they had him laced onto that pony's back tighter than a woodtick on a wolf's tail.

Before Jesse could begin to guess at the reason for Tim's captivity, the renegade had ridden on past, closely followed by his special and delighted guard, the perpetually grinning Skull. Regardless of his puzzlement, the mountain man knew that the ropes which bound Tim's feet beneath his mount's potbelly must have an explanation which very probably concerned him, Jesse, most personally, As Skull and the captive white man passed, Jesse knew that his first problem had just been put—the discovery of what lay behind Tim's fall from grace.

Strung out for a quarter-mile back of the white man and his leering guard, eating the rising gray trail dust of the others, straggled the main pack of Watonga's flea-bitten coyotes. Watching the last of them disappear over the top of a mile-distant rise, Jesse let out his breath, eased off on Heyoka's nosewrap.

"By God, Old Clown," he muttered, feelingly, "they're riding just right—heading to hook up with the village and not a scout or outrider in the lot of them. *Hookahey*, Heyoka! Let's get out of here!"

The mountain man spent the first part of that night on a hogback ridge six hundred feet above the fully rejoined Arapaho village. The lodge fires were lit early and Jesse could see from the distant movement of the tiny figures toward Watonga's central tipi that a powwow of some kind was coming up. To get closer he decided to risk a roundabout sneak-up on the council gathering. There was never any telling what a Sioux reared man could make out from sight-reading the fluent Indian handsigns and keeping an ear cocked for the louder bursts of red oratory. If he could get in close enough, he might learn plenty.

He had good luck. A spur of the very ridge he was on ran clear down into the campsite, being close to twenty feet high where it ended in among the tipis, and heavily covered with low brush. He was able to get up to within fifteen yards of Black Coyote's open-air Indian forum.

Watonga and his six subchiefs were squatted around a blazing fire, chewing the last of the pemmican and discussing such varied topics as the lack of heavy buffalo sign, the best way to boil a fat dog and, naturally, the legal status and problematical future hunting grounds of an erstwhile friendly white man suspect of having turned traitor in the small matter of the recent abortion of the attempt to wipe out the emigrant train.

Jesse held his breath at this mention of Tim, waiting shadow-quiet for Watonga to proceed.

Presently the chief spoke to Gray Bear.

"Go and get him, now."

Gray Bear nodded to Elk Runner and the two friends departed to return in a moment with the bound and glowering Tim O'Mara stalking between them. A quick look around the fire changed the renegade's expression from one of anger to one of uneasy apprehension. And with excellent reason.

Yellow Leg was there and he was a reassuring sight, his shriveled parchment face, snake's eyes and dwarfed leg toting up to a sum of rare comfort. Blood Face squatted next to him, a still pleasanter vision, the birthmark which gave him his name spreading its sick stain from his forehead well past his loose, purple lips. Dog Head was pretty, too. And well named. His jaw and nose were long, and his mouth began up by his ears and featured four hand-filed canines which glistened attractively whenever he chose to smile. Which was about once every three years. Toad was equally winning, his bloated body, neckless head and thick, warted skin giving ample evidence of the logic behind the name.

The last, and in size, least, of Watonga's headmen was the most cheerful of the lot. Not one of the subchiefs, this brave squatted well back from the others. The handful of dry twigs which Yellow Leg threw on the fire at the approach of Tim O'Mara flared to reveal his heretofore unnoticed presence to Jesse. His tall, elegantly proportioned comrades called him, simply, Skull.

Very short for an Arapaho, Skull's continual, racking cough was the clue to the dread White Man's Plague which accounted for his skeletonlike emaciation. The broad, Mongol structure of his face, whence came his name, wore a perpetual delighted grin. The fact that this expression was the result of jaw muscles contorted in their healing from a Comanche lance slash did nothing to detract from Skull's bright outlook. He appeared incapable of harming a weanling mouse, would open his mother's guts for a fair horse or a handful of good powder. Skull was a war-raid orphan, adopted by Watonga himself. He was only nineteen, the best tracker and bloodiest knife-fighter in the band, and Black Coyote's prime court favorite.

There were no introductions as Tim's guardians stepped back to give him the firelit central stage.

"What has Big Face to say?" In his hiding place, Jesse marked the fact the Indians had a familiar name for the renegade, judging from this that Brigham Young's mission was not his first work among them. "We trusted you," Watonga was continuing, "and you betrayed us. Do you deny it?"

The Arapaho chief had addressed his question in Sioux, the common language of all the Plains Tribes, and to Jesse's continuing education, Tim answered them in the pure, fluent tongue. Evidently, little Johnny O'Mara had known what he was talking about when he'd told Jesse Tim knew as much about Indians as he did.

"*Wonuncun*," waved the renegade, using the Sioux apology word. "A mistake has been made. I don't even know what you are talking about."

"All right, I'll tell you," grinned Watonga. "We agreed, you and me, to steal that gunpowder for the Mormon chief. Then

83

this white Sioux, this Tokeya Sha, was too clever for us at the Gully of the Jackpines. He fooled you, too, when you waited for him in the trail with Bear Gall and Walks-His-Horse and High Wolf. Is my tongue straight, brother?"

"*He-hau*," Tim nodded quickly, the puzzled Sioux affirmative followed by an anxious, "but what has this to do with a betrayal, cousin?"

"Nothing. Not a thing—" Black Coyote's eloquent shrug put the Indian lie to his feigned indifference.

"Well—?"

"Well, then my squaw, Ousta, going late last night to the bathing pool for water, was in time to hear your woman tell Tokeya Sha she would leave you and run away with him. Ousta came away quickly to tell you this, making your heart very bad for Tokeya Sha and your woman."

"Aye," Tim's square jaw jutted with remembered venom, "and we made an agreement, you and me. To attack my wagons and seize my woman."

"Very true, " Watonga nodded, pleasantly. "You said you cared nothing for the woman but that you would take her and sell her among the Comanches to poison this Tokeya's heart. And you said that in return for helping you attack the shabby *Wasicun* goddams, you would promise me two big things. You would see that Ousta should have the red-headed boy to rear in Watonga's tipi. You would give us a new plan to steal the gunpowder for the Mormon chief. *Nohetto!*"

"These are true words, cousin, but where is your betrayal?" The sweat streams brimming the dirt-choked channels of the white man's thick neck rose not from the warm night alone. "We agreed and you attacked, that's all!"

"Not quite, brother—" The slit-eyed denial fell flatly. "We agreed and I attacked, yes. But as I attacked here again came that cursed Tokeya Sha, and this time with many white rifles. I left twelve good warriors, quiet there in the Grass of the Wild Horses. Now, brother, I did not tell that red-haired Sioux I was going to attack him. Ousta did not tell him. So, then, answer this, Big Face. *How did Tokeya Sha know about that attack!*"

Jesse could see Tim was as stunned by the turn of events as he, Jesse, by learning for the first time of the full charge of the renegade's treachery.

Tim looked helplessly about him, began stumblingly to talk. Sure the noble chiefs could see that he had no way to *prove* he knew nothing of how Tokeya Sha had come into

84

the knowledge of Watonga's plan for the attack on the emigrants. They would just have to believe that Big Face's tongue was straight, as it had always been with his red brothers. As to the new plan for seizing the gunpowder, he had really had one. But then Watonga had seized him and made him prisoner and would not let him talk of it.

As the renegade went along, his red fellows began nodding and grunting, pleasantly. Tim took heart. It was clear that he was still the old master at befuddling these red half-wits. Why, they were all as simple-minded as so many settlement goofs. All a man had to do was have guts and a gift for gab. Tim had guts enough to stuff a bear, with maybe a handful left over. As for gab, he never ran out of that. It was plain that he still had the gullible buzzards firmly in hand. Secure in this belief, he wound up his speech abruptly.

When he finished, Watonga took one step. Right out of that hand.

"Well, well. Now that you have spoken, here is what I think. Big Face stinks like a sick dog."

Tim had time to gasp and that was all.

"Let us understand one another, brother," Black Coyote continued softly. "I say that you never had another plan for seizing the powder and that you plotted with Tokeya Sha to trap us in that meadow so that you could take all the powder and supplies for yourselves."

"Black Coyote is an idiot!" Tim's words burst angrily. "Where is the sense in such a plan? This Tokeya had stolen my woman. He is a faithful friend of Big Throat's.* I have been well paid by the Mormon chief. I—"

Watonga interrupted the interrupter.

"Who can make sense out of the ways of white men? We think Big Face is a liar, and we no longer trust him. I think we will kill him, too."

"How will we do it?" asked Skull, happily.

"I'd like to burn his feet first," suggested Yellow Leg, amicably. "Like the Utes burned this leg of mine."

"No, no," Blood Face put in, hurriedly. "Too simple. There is no art in burning like that."

"That's right," Dog Head agreed. "No art in that."

"How about just taking the tongue out?" asked Elk Runner. "I mean before the other things, of course. That always feels good."

---

* Another of the Plains Indians' names for Jim Bridger.

"Yes," his friend Gray Bear sided in, earnestly. "And we could flay the tongue first. You remember how that Kiowa showed us last summer. You heat the hot grease until it is blue, and then—"

"Enough!" snapped Watonga. "We'll leave it to my woman, Ousta. She'll know how to remind a white brother who gives our plans away and lets us be trapped like wet-nosed children. Ousta has a head for such things. That squaw's a real artist. She'll know how to do it best."

"Yes, nobody like Ousta for fun. I'm thinking that, too." Skull was trying to be helpful.

"No matter what you think," barked Black Coyote, "any of you. It will be as I say. We will leave here tomorrow and go on after the buffalo. After we have found a herd and made our winter meat, we'll have a dance with Big Face. *Nohetto,* that's all."

Jesse didn't need Black Coyote's final word to tell him that Tim was flayed closer than a new-skinned skunk. When the Arapaho got their buffalo hunting done, they would set up a scalp dance, a real *Pekocan sunpi wacipi.* It was the season for such affairs. And when the last ceremony was over, Tim would have tripped the light fantastic right on through the front ballroom of *Wanagi Yata,* the Indian Land of the Final Shadow.

As for Tim, the former wagon guide for the Kansas emigrants and sometime Mormon jack-of-all-dirty-trades was thinking of how he had never learned to dance. And of how he would hate like tarnal sin to take his first lesson from Watonga and his Wind River Arapaho.

All the next day, Jesse trailed the slow-moving village, the welcome shade of twilight bringing him and his Indian quarry out onto the main Medicine Road. As he watched the scattered caravan crowd out of the rough country and line out on the broad, wheel-rutted track of the Oregon Trail, the new direction of the hostiles' line-of-march, together with the leisurely trail gait with which they headed into it, brought a grunt of satisfaction from the mountain man.

Scanning the dusty southward reach of the trail behind the Arapaho cavalcade, he caught the distant glimmer of the jagged Green River range which marked the site of Fort Bridger. *Wagh!* Plenty good, by damn. Gabe's peaks. Everything was smack-dab on the schedule he had given Morgan Bates and his Missouri skinners. It brought a good feeling inside a man to find his tricky Indian arithmetic came toting up to a surefire sum.

The red buzzards were heading north, taking the wide-open Medicine Road while they were about it, and traveling plum slow. *And at this point they weren't three days' mule drive above Gabe's Fort!*

Later that evening, Jesse, shivering in the nightcold of his fireless hiding place above the Indian camp, had time for a little more frontier sum-toting. The answer came out that if Andy Hobbs had hammered his mules from first light to late dark, every day since Morgan and the boys had gotten back to him with the emigrant survivors, he might now be at Fort Bridger. That would put the arrival of the powder wagon to Jesse's present position at about four, probably five, days away.

Cripes! A man would need some luck, now.

If Watonga headed up the Medicine Road by regular marches, even not hurrying his present pace any, the powder wagon *still* could miss ever catching up to him. And if he headed west, into the goat-tangle of the Wasatches, it *sure* never would.

It was a spot for some big luck and fast figuring. Depending on what action daylight brought from Black Coyote, Jesse might have to move on in and make his lone-hand stab at snatching Lacey's boy away from him.

What daylight did bring was neither of the things the mountain man feared—it was worse than both of them.

With sunup, the nervestrung trapper saw all the lodges, save one, come tumbling down. By eight o'clock, the main village had departed, moving straight up the Medicine Road in long marching order. Left behind, were Watonga's stark-black hunting tipi and his hundred hard-core warriors.

This war-painted remainder made no move to travel, lolling around the deserted camp until close to high noon. Jesse had not been able to see Johnny among the multi-ponied panoply of the departing village but an hour ago he'd spotted Ousta coming out of the chief's lodge and had guessed from this, with a sense of vast relief, that the boy hadn't left with the main tribe.

With the sun directly overhead, things picked up down below, Watonga appearing in full hunting garb to lead his restless pack through the yelling ceremony of a short Buffalo Stomp.

Jesse's interest perked, at once. By cripes, this was more

like it. Evidently, this was a picked group of hunters, hanging back while the main bunch drifted to the Wind River winter camp. He should have guessed as much from the fact they kept no lodges, and from the hefty size of the horse herd that stayed with them. You needed plenty of ponies to run meat and tote beef, happen you got into a good bunch of young cows.

Now, if the sons would only lay around camp a couple of days to give the powder wagon a chance to get up from Fort Bridger.

The mountain man had no more than put the wish that they would into his head, than he saw Watonga's black lodge coming down. Minutes later, the whole passel of them were streaming off west, nearly square away from the Medicine Road, into a country where a wagon could go, easy— providing it could fly.

Jesse knew this country. The track led up toward Portola Springs, through Carson's Canyon by way of the Rockpile Meadow. It was the direct route to Coulter's Meadow,* the famed North Park of the Rockies, where buffalo could be found when they weren't any place else in the Indian world.

Riding hard, the mountain man got uptrail of the savage column, tied Heyoka in an alder clump, and bellied his way up over the trail where it squeezed through a narrow granite defile leading into Carson's Canyon. Here he could all but spit on the braves as they filed past beneath him. Plenty close, anyway, to check for certain sure if they had Johnny with them.

He had to *know* that. He couldn't just guess at it.

Ten minutes later, Watonga's lump-jawed face came bobbing over a ridgetop a hundred yards away. The chief topped-out on the ridge, started haunchsliding his pony down into the declivity above which Jesse lay. After him piled the grim train of his followers, *headed by Ousta and Johnny O'Mara.*

When the woman and the boy passed below him, Jesse noted the youngster was drawn-looking, no longer chipper and whistling. Looking at the brute faces of his Arapaho escorts, the mountain man could understand the change.

The kid might be spunky enough, but the first excitement was gone. No doubt he had expected his white folks to catch the Indians and get him away from them long before this.

---

* The hostiles' "Cheyenne Mesa."

More specifically, he probably had looked for "Tokeya, the Minniconjou" to come thundering out of the sunset and kill every last one of these mangy red dogs, releasing "Red Eagle" amid a withering hail of gunfire and high-pressure Sioux screaming. Now, three days of hard trailing through a lonely wilderness, with no sign of a conquering white hero anyplace, had silenced the boy.

He was a pinched-faced, scared-looking kid when he jogged past below Jesse on the little spotted pony. The mountain man's heart turned over in him with a heavy tug that lumped his throat proper. Mister, if he didn't get that boy away from Watonga and his slate-faced wife, it wouldn't be for not trying.

Waiting for the Arapaho to get on past, Jesse got his second jolt. At the tail of the bunch, flanked by Yellow Leg and Dog Head, followed by the set-grinning Skull, came the bound and scowling Tim O'Mara.

The captive renegade, eyes red from spending his nights laced upright against a tree, a long week's trail dust blurring his slabface, buckskins dirt-stinking from not having been off of him in six suns, looked about as happy as a short-haired hound in a bluestone hailstorm.

Raising his head and shifting his body to get a better look, Jesse's hand moved a fraction. A walnut-sized pebble rattled over the edge of the rimrock, fell toward the passing Indians.

At the first rattle, Tim's nervous eyes snapped upward, the slit glances of his red companions following swiftly.

Jesse jerked his head back down, lay tense and ear tuned. A cat couldn't have been any more strung up to jump. Cuss it all, why did a man have to get careless just when his chances were near snowed, anyway? Tim had seen him, sure as the devil's chimney had a hot flue, and likely the rest of the infernal slanteyes, too.

The guttural questions barked up from below did nothing to loosen the bite of the mountain man's nails in the scaly granite of the rimrock.

"What was that?" Yellow Leg's challenge burst, growlingly.

"I heard nothing," smiled Skull. "Only a pebble rattling down. A lizard, maybe. Who would know?"

"I would!" snapped Dog Head. "I thought I saw something get back of that rock, up there. It was bright, like hair. I'm going up there."

Jesse's belly shrank and the spittle dried in his mouth. He

89

gathered himself to leap and run for it. Tim, bass voice sneering, spared him the jump.

"Sure it was hair. I saw it. An old boar marmot. Very bright color, almost red. Big as a man's head. He went right behind that rock, like Dog Head says. That one you are pointing at, there, Dog Head. Didn't you see it, cousin?"

"I don't know. It looked too red, not gray enough for a whistle dog." Dog Head was obdurate, inspiring Jesse to give Tim's surprising co-operation a gentle boost. He hadn't tried the trick since he was a boy with Waniyetula, but there'd been a time not even Winter Boy, that prairie magician of animal imitations, could beat Tokeya at whistling up marmots. Pouching his taut cheeks, he brought the breath high and jerky through his clenched teeth.

"Ho, ho! You hear that, you dogface, you?" Yellow Leg was laughing at his comrade. "It is even as Big Face said. An old dog whistler, nothing more. Come on, we fall too far back. Watonga wants to pitch his lodge at those springs tonight. *Hopo. Hookahey!*"

"All right," Dog Head gave in, grumblingly. "*Hopo*. It was too red, though. Way too red."

When they had gone, Jesse rolled back off the rimrock, legged it for Heyoka. Mounting up, he raced the gray mare back toward Medicine Road and the previous night's Indian Camp.

There, twenty minutes' work with his knife, and some cookfire charcoal on the back of his buckskin shirt, and he had done all he could to steer Morgan Bates and the hoped-for mule skinners. When he swung back up on Heyoka, kicking her around for Carson's Canyon again, the shirt stayed behind, flapping on a cottonwood stake jammed into the broad trace of the main Medicine Road.

Happen a stray gang of redskins didn't wander along to tear it down, meantime, a pack of white teamsters from Fort Bridger, providing they moseyed this way and could read Sioux sign scratching, might get the idea that at this point in the Medicine Road, Tokeya the Minniconjou had lit out toward Rockpile Meadow, hot on the tracks of a big black coyote and a very small red eagle.

Tim O'Mara, the renegade Mormon, was well born into a big trade. Strong as a buffalo, tough as a range bull, tricky as a fox in a farmer's barnyard, moral as a stray dog, Tim was bred to get fat grazing trouble's lean pasture.

90

You get yourself a bad lot like that snubbed up to where his string is shorter than a broken breech-cloth lace, and you can dig your toes in for some fast shuffles.

In the case of the old boar marmot diving behind that rock back there on the canyon rim, Tim had seen enough to know that Dog Head had been right. That marmot had been way too bright-colored. Too bright-colored and red-haired. Too narrow-eyed and sunburned. Too wide-mouthed and human-looking.

Tim's first impulse had been to yell out and put Jesse Callahan out of business for good. His second thought, plugging his big-lipped mouth tighter than the bung in a powder barrel, had been that the hidden white man represented what might be his last link with the world of safety. A world which was currently falling behind Tim's scalp-itch-inspired rehabilitation at a shuffling pony gait of thirty miles a day.

At the moment Tim had no idea how he was going to profit by his knowledge that Jim Bridger's redheaded wagon guide was trailing Black Coyote's buffalo hunters. But the dry breast of necessity always has a mouthful of milk for the nurser who draws hard enough. By the time the Arapaho had stopped to give their ponies a noon-rest in Rockpile Meadow, he had it figured pretty close.

There could only be one reason for the mountain man's presence. He meant, somehow, to sneak in and release that damn brat of Lacey's. And that gave Tim his idea.

The idea was a revolutionary one for a total bad man, but Tim O'Mara was a born revolutionist. If he, Tim, could some way beat Jesse Callahan to that triumph, could in some way manage to free the boy and return him to the white settlements, he would be in a position to share in some of the humpfat of heroism which would undoubtedly reward that rescue.

The hog's bulk of Tim's body was free of the fat of sentiment. The Mormon hireling would as quickly have shot the boy as saved him. Providing the pay was better that way. As it was, if he could get the captive boy out of the Arapaho camp, Tim would be as welcome in the white settlements as salt in a thin stew. And not only welcome but in all likelihood pardoned for his apparent part in the Horse Bend massacre.

As far as his own bulging neck went, Tim was gambling less than nothing in any attempt he might make to free Lacey's boy. His Arapaho "brothers" were carrying him along only until they might find the time to serve him up in style—the Indian taste for traitor meat being what it was. On this score the captive white man had no illusions. Nor was the worry attendant on that score any great problem. The only problem in Tim's whole sly world at the moment was how to break away with that little red-haired dripnose of Lacey's.

Come sundown that afternoon at Portola Springs, that problem would be taken care of, too. And along this latter line, the Mormon had some particular ideas. . . .

Skull, his constant guard, had always had a sort of mutual, rascal's admiration for the squat renegade. In matters of tactical execution: the business of how best to incise a scalpskin for the neatest removal of the hair; how, most cleanly, to cut a live victim's tongue out, or burn his toes off while not damaging the main foot in the least; how, with the greatest efficiency to open an opponent's bowels in dark-of-the-moon knife fighting, and such other little vital niceties of frontier survival, the settlement-bred Big Face was an acknowledged genius.

In his youthful, fresh way, Skull looked up to Tim. His was the clean-cut, clear-eyed, inspired admiration of the ambitious tyro for the finished master-butcher.

Of late, this touching admiration of Skull's had taken the course of allowing his bull-shouldered charge camp freedom at the end of the day's ride. At the same time, Tim was not entirely dazzled by this generous treatment. To the student of red psychology of Tim's rank, the motives of Watonga's protégé in this apparent kindly action must bear yet a bit more probing.

There was always the matter of courting the Big Coup.

Bored with the routine dullness of mothering a doomed captive, helpless and with his feet tied, the young brave had begun turning Tim loose in the hope the desperate white man might make a break for freedom. Though it went by the name of "Comanche Charity" among the Plains Tribes, "Ley Fuge," by any other name . . . was the same law. A prisoner ran—he got shot. And *Nohetto!* There you were. Oh, maybe not shot. Maybe knifed. Or lanced. Or skull-clubbed. Whatever looked like the most fun at the moment. Anyway, killed.

And with that, *wagh!* You had your coup. Always remembering that where the guard was a young man without particular reputation, and the prisoner was a rascal of Big Face's considerable record, it wasn't just an ordinary one. It was the Big Coup.

The Arapaho surprised the captive emigrant guide by halting early, five miles short of Portola Springs. Surprised and delighted him.

An advance scout party had ridden back from Crow Mesa, a high, barren grassland which formed one wing of Coulter's Meadow, with the news of a fine herd. Watonga had ordered his lodge up on the spot. Called an immediate council.

After a brief session with his subchiefs, it was decided not to try for the buffalo until tomorrow. Meat and powder were both too low. No chances of a hurried or careless stalk were to be considered.

Gray Bear and Elk Runner, the senior hunters, were sent out to tail the herd and figure the best plan for tomorrow's hunt. The rest of the camp busied itself readying weapons, cutting favored ponies out of the horse herd, staking them close in to the cooking fires for quick use in the morning. Old Pte was best hunted in the misty hours, and from the backs of fresh, strong ponies.

The unexpected confusion of preparation wasn't the only smile of fortune ready for the hapless Tim.

Johnny O'Mara was kept pretty much to Watonga's lodge, within hand's reach of the fierce red foster mother. In this camp, the chief's lodge had been pitched against a heavy fringe of cedar timber—timber which stretched unbroken along the canyon's floor for the back four miles of trail. And now, Ousta was hustling overtime, completely busy with the dressing of the last of the meat and the heating of the *tunkes** for the pre-hunt feast.

There was but a short half-hour of weak daylight remaining. If Tim could elude Skull, snatch Johnny out of Black Coyote's lodge and get into the dark timber it might go many minutes before either fugitive was missed. Minutes in which fast horses could be snaked out of the pony herd. Snaked out and scrambled astride of. Scrambled astride of and kicked in the rump. And quirted for their scrubby lives down the back-trail.

Given twenty minutes' start, full night would come before any considerable pursuit could catch up mounts and get on the trail. And given full night and two fast ponies, Tim would smile about his chances of keeping Watonga's coyotes from

---

* Red-hot stones, dropped in the paunch-skin cooking bags to heat the water for boiling meat.

cornering him and Lacey's kid. He was a real lad, Tim O'Mara. One with a big head. The marrow fat in those sly skullbones had greased his way out of more than one narrow squeak in his twenty-odd years of dealing with such as Black Coyote. *Woyuonihan!*

With daylight, once well away from his pursuers, he and Johnny could hole up, riding nights only. Or even walking, if it came to that. In any event, making it safely into old Bridger's fort with the cussed kid alive and unharmed. If they should encounter Jesse Callahan along the escape trail, all right. If they didn't, all right, too. Either way, the desperate long bow which the renegade had drawn on his chance to avoid certain destruction at the hands of his former red fellows, and to win a haven of safety and forgiveness with the frontier whites at Fort Bridger would bury its arrow to the fletching in the fleeting and tricky target of complete success.

Hun-hun-he! Pay the Brave Honors to Tim O'Mara, you red *heyokas*. There was a real chief, that Big Face. Even if he had to say it himself!

The condemned Mormon could see the holes in the blanket of his plan quite easily. They were as plain as the pock pits on a Pawnee's nose. Even so, a man in Tim O'Mara's position couldn't look too closely at a plot's complexion. Given one was dealing with captors like Ousta and Watonga, his best chance in a year of waiting wouldn't pile any higher than two bone-dry buffalo chips.

When Skull finally untied him to let him off the pony, Tim put on a good act of being mortally weary. Crawling weakly over to it, he collapsed beside a down log whose butt lay hidden in the fringing woods not thirty paces from Black Coyote's lodge. In turning around three times, like a choosy dog before lying down, the captive was careful to select a final spot where his outflung right hand lay less than inches away from a broken cedar snag thick as a man's wrist, two feet long, sun-dried to iron hardness.

Skull, lance-scar grin going full blast, idled over and slumped on the far side of the log.

A great actor, Skull. One of the best. In twenty seconds his snores were rattling the cones off half the cedars in the forest. Back of the snores, his pouchy eyes showed a hairline slit of glittering pupil between the heavy-closed lids. *Wagh*, so what of it? Skull always slept with the eyes a little open.

To Tim, lying panther-tight on the far side of the log, it made no difference if Skull were really asleep or not.

The renegade's eyes flicked left, out across the busy camp, right, over to the chief's deserted lodge, back again to the cedar chunk at his slack fingertips.

Skull had time to pop his eyes open—if not his mouth.

The cedar chunk bounced off his parchment-wrinkled temple, backed by an arm and shoulder of bearlike power and weight. Skull went down behind the log, scarred grin working wide and loose, empty eyes staring straight up, dead as a water rat in a blacksnake's belly.

Tim shaded thirty seconds getting over that log, grabbing Skull's trade musket and knife. Bellying into the cedar tangle, he catfooted his way up to the back of Watonga's lodge. Once there, the business of slitting the rear skins and popping through into the lodge's interior added another five seconds.

"Psstt! Shut up, Johnny!" he hissed at the startled boy. "It's me, Tim. Come on, boy. You and me are getting out'n here. You grab my shirttail and foller along. Jump it, now, and no noise!"

Johnny, rolling up off the pile of buffalo robes he'd been lying on, started crawling toward the waiting Tim. Halfway, he stopped, felt inside the front of his faded shirt, started crawling back toward the robes.

Tim was after him like a lightstreak, nailing him as he reached the furry pile. "You crazy little birdbrain! What're you up to? One mortal peep out'n you, boy, and I'll brain you! You got that?"

"I ain't going to peep, Tim," the boy whispered. "I got to get something. It must've slid out of my shirt—" He was rummaging in the robes as he talked, coming up shortly with a bright Green River skinning blade. "Here it is, Tim. See?"

"Come on, boy. Crawl after me. And remember, you make a sound and we're both shot and sculped."

Johnny nodded, big-eyed, scrambling across the lodge floor to follow his rescuer through the knifeslit. His feet were just disappearing through it when the tipi entrance behind him grew black against the graying twilight.

In Ousta's hand was a short stone maul used in pounding the dried buffalo before throwing it into the paunch skin to boil. Indianwise, the squaw made no outcry, slipped back out the front flap of the lodge and on around its side, gliding soundlessly as some monstrous black ferret.

The Arapaho woman had not seen Tim; expected only to

startle the white boy in a clumsy escape try. The training of a chief's son could not begin too early. Ya Slo must be taught that a good warrior always looked to his rear the last thing. She came powder-stepping around the lodge as the Mormon, meaning to carry the excited boy the first part of the way, was swinging Johnny over his shoulder.

With the game in full sight, Ousta broke her silence. The first hint Tim had that his scheme had lost the blessing of Wakan Tanka was the explosive grizzly snarl of the Arapaho war challenge. This cry, patterned after the coughing roar of the wounded silvertip, short, harsh, deep bass, was like no other sound on the plains. Hearing it, the white renegade wheeled in time to see the immense squaw towering over him, buffalo maul back-swung for the real coup.

Tim O'Mara's erratic mind was faulty only on the longer hauls. In short spells it worked like gun grease in a dry barrel. Rolling backward, he twisted the slight form of the boy between himself and the striking squaw. Ousta, swerving her falling arm to avoid braining Johnny, was thrown off balance.

Instantly the burly Mormon had her locked in a bear grip, the two of them rolling and growling in the flying cedar needles with all the fury of fighting dogs.

Johnny, scudding free of the tangle, dove for the sanctuary of the tipi-slit, making it just as Watonga and a dozen braves swept around the lodge.

Their arrival saved nobody's skin but Tim O'Mara's. Unable to unsheath the knife he had stolen from Skull, he had lost his own grip on Ousta's maul arm. The raging squaw was on the point of pulverizing the renegade's head when Black Coyote and his warriors piled into the melee.

It took a good half of the braves to seize and subdue Ousta, the remaining half surrounding the recumbent Tim. The white man lay where he was, making a noble effort not to twitch an eye, knowing the least move might put his trigger-nerved, erstwhile business associates on top of him.

The squaw was raving out her story to Watonga, and when she had finished the huge chief nodded to the Mormon.

"You heard the woman, Big Face. But you tell great stories, too. Good for a laugh, always. So talk, now. Now it is your turn. A laugh is never bad before food. Go on. Our ears are uncovered. Let the braves have a laugh before they put their lances through your liver."

Tim ran his eyes around his audience, found it creepily

96

attentive. Licking his thick lips, he arose and stepped forward, raising his right arm in the gesture used to request polite listening.

The glitter-eyed circle laughed, nodded the one to the other. *Waste,* good. Old Big Face was all right. He wasn't going to cheat them. He was a real talker. A real windbag. And no *can'l wanka,* no coward. Not Big Face. *H'g'un,* courage, Big Face! Go on.

In the moment of silence before he began talking, the Mormon traitor made his gamble and played it. It was dark now. Skull's death might well go unnoticed until morning. He had cached his guardian's gun back in the timber, had his knife hidden under his shirt. *Wagh!* All a man had left now was his mouth.

"I grew lonely with only Skull to be with. None of you, my true cousins, would talk to me. A lonely man longs for talk. And then I thought of the boy in the tipi. My heart is big for a man-child, like any Arapaho's. That big. This Ousta will let no one near the boy. And as you know, this boy is the son of my white squaw. I thought the boy would want to talk, too, to hear his own tongue. Skull left me, saying he was going back in the timber and make a Buffalo Dream for tomorrow. Skull honors me. You all know that. So I gave him my honor-word. But I was lonely. So I came to the boy. The squaw was working in front, so I had to come in the back. *Nohetto,* there you are!"

The braves looked at one another, scowling their disappointment. *Iho!* Well, well! Big Face was failing in his old age. No laugh here. Just a straight tongue. Too simple. No imagination. Any man could get lonely around that cursed Skull. Naturally. They shifted their gazes to Black Coyote, awaiting his word.

"Where is Skull?" asked the chief, presently.

"Off in the trees, like I said," shrugged the renegade. "Gone to make his dream. He said he would stay in the trees until first light, making a *big* dream. He said the need for meat was that bad. That he thought Black Coyote needed a real dream for tomorrow's hunt." Tim paused, assaying the effect of his tale on the blank-faced braves. Apparently the assay ran a little short. Clearly feeling this, the Mormon nervously fattened it up a bit. "Oh, and yes. Skull was going to see to his ponies. Going to bring them up from the herd for tomorrow. Right after the dream he was going to do that."

It was a good try, worthy of the politician's brain bequeathed Tim by his Hibernian forebears, and it had several of the braves nodding their understanding of such a serious business. Dreams were big things. Very important. Perhaps Black Coyote should reconsider his decision to let Ousta put this Big Face on the Red Holy Pole. After all, the need for meat *was* great. And if Skull's dreams were successful—

The nods had barely started when Dog Head's long jaw opened to snap them into instant motionless. "He had already brought his ponies up. I helped him."

"Go get Skull," ordered Watonga, his eyes studying the way the white man's skin was going gray under his travel-dust cover while the little silence born of Dog Head's blunt statement was living its brief moment and dying. "We will leave it to Skull. But be careful. If he is truly in a dream, don't wake him. He can talk later."

Yellow Leg and Dog Head were back in less than a minute.

"Skull won't talk for a long time," vouchsafed the former. "Not for a very long time."

"Not for any time," added the latter, succinctly.

"Where did you find him?" asked Black Coyote, softly.

"Back of the log where he lay down with Big Face," explained Yellow Leg. "He won't need all those ponies he brought up, now. Just one."

"His best one," agreed Dog Head, reverently. "That the journey to *Wanagi Yata* may be swift and pleasant."

"*Aii-eee!*" Watonga's sibilant answering hiss wasn't so low but what the pain in it was evident. Skull, for all his consumptive shortcomings, had been the light of the chief's fierce eye. "Anything else?"

"His gun was gone. The knife, too. You know that knife? The one with the white handle and the black skull burned on it? *Wagh!* I always wanted that knife—" Yellow Leg's suspended words took the eyes of all to the putty-faced Tim O'Mara.

By this time, the rest of the braves had come up from the cooking fires to crowd soundlessly behind the Mormon's accusers. In the silence Watonga stepped forward, put his hand inside the white man's hunting shirt, stepped back to hold aloft the bone handled, skull-emblazoned signature on Tim's death warrant.

His words spilled like glacier water down the rigid channel of the Mormon's spine.

98

"We will give him to my woman now. She caught him," was all he said. But as to the manner and immediacy of Tim's demise he couldn't have said more had he orated all night.

The squaw, who had retrieved Johnny O'Mara from the tipi, handed the child to Watonga, shifted the blunt-stoned maul to her right hand, stepped toward the waiting white captive. The braves pulled silently back, making a lance-studded circle.

Halfway across this circle, the crouching Ousta hesitated, interrupted by a commotion in the back rank of watching braves. The outer warriors parted to admit a newcomer, all eyes flicking in his direction.

Blood Face was excited, his silence-gesture sweeping dramatically with the barking "*A-ah!*" which announced his arrival. It was the tribal warning-word of sudden danger and it commanded precedence over even a traitor-killing.

"I was tracking Mato, Kicking Bear, my best buffalo pony. He wandered back along the canyon trail from whence we came today. The light was going bad and so were the tracks. But I saw those other tracks. The light wasn't that bad—"

"What other tracks?" Watonga's question was instant and intense.

"*Shacun* moccasin. Toed-in."

"Snake!" the name burst from a dozen slit-mouths, labeling the enemy people, the Shoshone.

"Not Shoshone!" Blood Face's contradiction was harsh. "Minniconjou! I know that track. I have studied it well. Do not forget, I was the last scout, before Toad, to leave that red-wheeled goddam's trail before the Gully of the Jackpines."

"Tokeya Sha!" Ousta snarled the hated name.

"Aye," nodded Blood Face. "Tokeya Sha, the Minniconjou."

Turning to await Watonga's word on Blood Face's startling discovery, the braves were interested to see the chief's huge jaw spreading the frost of a slow smile across his coarse features. "*Waste*," growled the hulking savage. "Good, good."

Blood Face had expected more than this out of the drama of his revelation and showed his irritation immediately. "How is this? I bring Watonga news of his great enemy. I tell him that Tokeya Sha is following him. And he does no more than

99

stand there grinning like a dog coyote smelling fresh calf blood!"

"I just thought of something," answered Watonga, letting the grin spread unchecked. "Let me ask you. Who gets the first rules of *Woyuonihan*? Even above the best friend?"

"The worst enemy," frowned Blood Face. "Any *heyoka* knows that."

"All right, then. We owe this Tokeya Sha hard Courtesy Rules. Am I talking straight?"

His answer was a wave of scowling nods.

Erasing his slack smile, Watonga added his own scowl to the others. "So, then. Who gave us this white mongrel in the first place? Who was it attacked our ambush in the Grass of the Wild Horses, thus letting us know of Big Face's treachery?" The chief's repeated questions were accompanied by glowering thumbstabs at the Mormon.

"Tokeya Sha, who else?" admitted Blood Face.

"Even so," nodded Watonga. "And is the Sioux Fox to outdo the Arapaho Coyote in the matter of simple *Woyuonihan?*"

By now, the listening braves were beginning to swing into the drift of the chief's shifty thinking, their big mouths slackening into a splattering of loose-lipped grins.

"Truly, it must not happen that way," said Yellow Leg, seriously. "Clearly, we cannot avoid this matter of courtesy. It must be as Watonga is thinking."

"Well?" Blood Face's growl showed all the resentment of the slow mind left behind by swifter ones. "What in Pte's name *is* Watonga thinking? I am lost as a blind wolf whelp six feet from a hind teat!"

Watonga's deep gutturals boomed out, giving the answer to them all. "When this stinking Big Face betrayed us for the first time, Tokeya Sha attacked us and so warned us of the betrayal. Now Big Face has betrayed us for the second time. He has tried to steal my little white son, Ya Slo. *Nohetto*, there you are. This time Watonga will leave Big Face in the middle of the trail for Tokeya Sha. It is *Woyuonihan*, Courtesy Rules, that's all."

Jesse, moving as close on Watonga's backside as a man dared in shut-in country, cast a worried eye skyward. Above the overhanging canyon escarpments, the sunglow was cooling out. Already, the gray of early evening was blurring the hostile pony tracks. Another five minutes, and a cat couldn't see that trail with glasses.

As it was, Jesse had to follow it afoot the last mile. And being off his horse, with the cussed Heyoka tied in a cedar clump a mile back there, didn't add to a man's easy breathing, either.

Owing to the brush-choked nature of the canyon, he'd had to hang farther back than he liked, too. In more open country a man could see to take his chances. In here, with the scrub and all, you had to tread mighty light and far back. One thing, anyway, he had plenty of room now.

The Arapaho would surely make Portola Springs their camp for tonight; were, no doubt, already there. That gave him a good six miles to play with. He'd sneak those miles plenty quick, once dark shut down, and be right on top of old Watonga when he broke camp next morning.

Rounding a blind corner in the narrow track, he nearly knocked heads with the fact he wouldn't have to wait until morning for Black Coyote.

He was on top of him right now.

The grazing Indian pony threw up his head, stood staring, prick-eared, nostrils flaring. The mountain man knew another second would bring the nervous animal the hated *Wasicun* scent, start him to whistling out the warning-whicker.

"*Waste, sunke wakan. Waste, waste!*" Jesse muttered the Indian words like a prayer, slipped back into the screening brush as he did so and crouched, breath-held, awaiting the little beast's reaction.

Confused by the familiar, gut-deep tongue, the pony hesitated; snuffled curiously, forgot its momentary alarm, fell to grazing again.

Seconds later, Blood Face trotted down the trail.

"Ho, there, Mato! May Wakan Tanka curse you with spavins and stringhalt. An hour in camp, and there you are two miles along the backtrail!"

The pony moved a few yards away from Blood Face, as the subchief came sidling up to seize its trailing halter rope. "Next time Watonga finds a herd of buffalo and calls an early camp, I'll stake you so close to the—" The brave's voice broke in mid-threat, his eyes going quickly to the thick dust of the trail a few paces beyond the pony. Only a second he hesitated, before swinging up on Mato and turning him for camp.

After all, when you're one of the best trackers on the

Short Grass, you don't need more than a second to single out a Sioux moccasin stamp from four hundred barefoot pony prints.

In his piñon-scrub cover, Jesse cursed. Had the red son seen his tracks, or hadn't he?

Chances were, he hadn't. The light was nearly gone and besides, what difference did it make? A man ought to be thanking Wakan Tanka that the Arapaho hadn't seen *him*, not fretting about whether he'd spotted his moccasin prints. As a matter of calm fact, the brave probably hadn't seen even those. Anyway, Jesse sure as sin hoped he hadn't. It was quirky enough trailing a hundred nervestrung hostiles, without they were on to you being after them.

Piecing together what he knew of the Carson's Canyon Trail with what the Arapaho subchief had hollered at his wandering pony, the mountain man figured Watonga must be camped in Carson's Creek Flats, two miles ahead, five short of Portola Springs. Also, that the reason for the halt had been the discovery of buffalo ahead. Blood Face had said so, and the subchief's word was good enough for Jesse.

Now, any sizeable herd would not be down in the canyon but up on Coulter's Meadow somewhere, beyond the springs. That was a ten-mile trot from Watonga's present camp. The sons would have to leave in the dark, tomorrow, probably about four, to get up on the herd by daylight.

The more he thought of it, the better it shaped up. The Indians would no doubt make their hunting camp at Portola Springs, leave Johnny and the squaw there to get ready for the meat-dressing. The hunters would likely be gone the best part of the day. Cripes, a man couldn't ask for a much better shot than looked to be coming up—a near-deserted camp, heavy timber, one squaw to handle, and ten hours to handle her in!

If a Minniconjou-trained gambler couldn't make a hand like that pay off, he'd just as well forget the whole game.

When Jesse snaked out of the brush to go dogtrotting back toward the hidden Heyoka, the set of his mouth and eyes were those of a man who had just drawn three cards to an inside straight—and made it.

Carson's Creek Flats lay like the bulge of a paunch skin in the slender channel of the canyon, the narrowed neck pointing toward Jesse. In this regard, the mountain man's approach to the Indian campsite, cautiously made about 5:00

a.m., was necessarily a blind one. There was no way to see into the Flats save to follow the main trail squarely on into them. Sneaking around the last turn in that trail, hand-leading Heyoka, Jesse's eyes widened.

The Indians were clean gone, all right, but they had left a little something behind for Tokeya Sha.

Its name was Tim O'Mara and it was rawhide-bound, hand and foot and stark naked, to a four-inch sapling stump in the center of the deserted clearing.

The first flash that tightened the trapper's tenderloins was that Watonga had built a *wickmunke* for him, using Tim as bait. Then, given a little thought, the idea of a trap didn't hold up too well. Even if Watonga knew he was after him, he had ought to know better than to try to bait Jesse with Tim. Or to bait him at all, after falling into Jesse's trap at Jackpin Slash.

By cripes, there was something fishier here than Friday in St. Patrick's parish.

In a spot like this, there was only one sure thing to do: circle the whole flats and make dead certain there wasn't a pack of Arapaho ambushed to jump him the minute he moseyed out to sniff around Tim.

Considering this long-head action, the preciousness of time forced him to chuck it out.

Carson's Creek Gorge cut into the main canyon here at the Flats from the east, its own canyon being nearly a quarter-mile wide at the junction. If a man circled the Flats, he would have to feel up that side canyon half a mile or so, too. By the time he'd got that done, he'd have shot two hours he didn't have to spare. And likely for nothing, at that.

Chances were near gut-cinched that the Arapaho had gone on, had tied Tim out naked with the idea of having him sunbake and thirst to death. It sure wasn't accident that the bubbling thread of Carson's Creek ran past just inches beyond the staked-out renegade's feet.

Crouching back in the trail-fringe brush, the mountain man calculated his next move. When a man had run a ten-to-one track into an odds-on stymie like this, he might as well chunk in the rest of his poke.

Leaving Heyoka in the brush, Jesse chunked his in.

Swiftly he went, gliding out into mid-clearing, bearing down on the waiting Tim like a mountain cat coming up on a tied-out colt. Eastward, the sun was just rimming the mesa, tumbling its red flood down the cedar-black gullet of Carson's Creek Gorge.

The hostiles had rigged Tim with what Jesse's Sioux folks called an Arapaho halter. This was an inch-wide strip of green rawhide, passed through the mouth, cinched down on the tongue and tied fast back of the skullbase. What this crude bit, shrinking slowly in the sun, did to discourage a man's urge to converse was six shades stiffer than considerable.

Even after Jesse had slashed it out of his mouth, Tim couldn't make anything but deaf-mute mumbles for a full minute. Then he got his tongue going.

"Listen, Callahan," delivered in hoarse earnest, the Mormon renegade's plea broke out desperately, "and for Gawd's sake, believe me—!"

"Go on!" snapped Jesse, blue eyes swinging an apprehensive circle around the Flats.

Now that he was out in the open, the mountain man's Indian hunch was hammering at him again, telling him he had likely been right, first off, thinking this thing was a hostile trap. Tim's rushing speech stumbled in, harsh and heavy, on his red-haired companion's rising instincts.

"They left me haltered like this for trying to get the kid away. I killed that lousy Skull, grabbed the boy and run for it. The squaw nailed me and would have killed me but for Black Coyote busting in. He thought it would be funny as all-get-out to leave me tied up for you to finish me off—"

"What are you trying to give me, O'Mara?" Jesse's interruption was ignited by the quick flash of the narrowed eyes behind it.

"Listen, I'm telling you. You know how them red scuts are for their crazy Courtesy Rules. Well, they somehow figured I had tipped you off to that ambush in Hoss Meadow. They give you credit for letting them know I'd crossed them up. So Watonga he says, *Wagh!* We'll leave Big Face, that's me, see, in the trail as a Courtesy Gift for Tokeya Sha!"

"Well—?" Jesse's challenge froze the perspiration beading Tim's scowling gaze.

"Well, hell, they figured you'd kill me account of them grabbing me when I took out after the squaw in Hoss Meadow and making it look like I was mixed up in the ambush."

"You know something, O'Mara—" The mountain man's break-in was deceptively quiet. "They figured *right!*"

"My Gawd, Callahan, you don't mean that! We're white men. Listen. Didn't I steer them off'n you when you knocked that pebble off the cliff? Didn't I try to—"

Jesse's answer came with the flashing knife blade which whipped out to sever Tim's bonds. "I'm cutting you loose. You get ten seconds to loosen up your arms and legs. Then I'm going to kill you, mister. With my hands."

Flexing his thick shoulders, the renegade shot a side glance at the waiting mountain man, decided to make one more try. "Callahan, I ain't lost no more love for you than you have for me. But unless I can have a hand in getting that kid of Lacey's back from them scuts, I ain't got a chance in the settlements. Leave me throw in with you. There's nobody in the camp up yonder but the kid and the squaw. The braves are all up on the mesa running buffler. I swear I ain't had nothing to do with this whole deal. As for Lacey, hell, you can have her. You got her, anyway. Me, I just don't want them red buzzards sticking me full of cedar needles and burning my hide off. What do you say, Callahan?"

If there was a time Jesse would have felt any kinship with the white man in front of him, it was long gone. He wasn't seeing Tim O'Mara's sweaty face, nor hearing his hoarse-growled words. He was seeing the sodden blanketed, egg-shell crush of little Kathy's head, and hearing the dull, sick monotone of her shocked mother's low-voiced cry, "Dead. Dead—"

"I say you're a liar, O'Mara. And that your ten seconds have come and gone."

"Callahan!"

"Save it," grated Jesse. "I was in that brush spur over Watonga's lodge when the subchiefs voted you down. It was a still night, mister, and none of you was whispering."

Jesse was backing off with his words, placing his Hawken and knifebelt carefully out of reach on a shelf-high rock ledge. He saw the dark light shoot Tim's sudden scowl at his flat challenge. Didn't miss the following blankness which spread like pond ice over the big Irishman's slab face. Knew, without anybody having to write him a letter about it, that he had made his match—and met it.

"You came after me once, O'Mara," was all he said, "now I'm coming after you—"

Tim's answer was to glide away from the mountain man's crouching advance, his light-stepping, easygoing way, as though his feet had better eyes in them than his head, letting Jesse know he had a *fighting* man on his hands.

And in the breath-held seconds of the first wary circling, a man had that strange, timeless pause which goes ahead of any hand-to-hand encounter where the announced stakes are life itself to study just how much of a fighting man!

Tim O'Mara was big. Six-two, anyway. And as thickset and well balanced as a boar grizzly. His massive, fleshy head was set on a neck that seemed to be nothing more than a foot-wide continuation of the sloping, ropy-muscled shoulders. His eyes, tiny and close-set as any bear's, appeared lost in the receding shadow cast over them by the protruding Neanderthal brow ridge. His wide, blunt jaw, slack now under the looseness of the thick lips above it, had the look and cut of base rock. A keg-chested, heavy-waisted man, his wide hips and thick legs were a grotesquely bulky foundation for the support and movement of the gross muscularity of the great trunk above them. Crouching, now, moving lightly, stripped to the gee-string as the Arapaho had left him, nearly the whole of his hulking figure overlaid with a coarse mat of black body hair, Tim O'Mara looked brute enough to give any fellow human ample pause.

Across from him moved a man of different cut. Not as tall as Tim, but lean, supple, graceful, Jesse Callahan was the Mormon renegade's diametric physical opposite; the kind of spare, unimposing-looking man an opponent would be likely to dismiss, at first glance, as ordinary.

Then, if that opponent were a seasoned frontier rough like Tim, he would take another look, as Tim was taking now, and figure maybe this mountain jasper wasn't so ordinary after all.

He was of medium stature, with a pair of high-set, flat-wide shoulders you could lay a coupstick handle across, and still not span. And a set of Missouri-size ham hands that were backed up with a brace of wrists as thick through and broad across as a bull buffalo's hocks. And what there was to the rest of him was pure, dry muscle and dense, big bone. He handled himself in a way that made you watch him, too. Feet moving as softly as though there were nothing but summer wind under his moccasin soles. Huge hands and forearms flexing and unflexing in that slow, rhythmic way that told you you'd better get in close to this one. Close and bearhug-tight. Where he couldn't wind up that rock-sized fist and throw it with that mule-muscled shoulder back of it.

106

And just about when you had settled your mind to that, you found yourself looking into the quietest face you'd ever seen on a man. And, back of the face, into the chilliest pair of blue-dark eyes this side of a High Sierra snowcap. And then you didn't know what to think. And you just kept on moving in your circle. Moving and watching. Watching and moving.

Five eternity-long seconds dragged away as Jesse deliberately closed the circle. He was within six feet of his man now. Another step and it was five. Then four. And still the big Mormon waited.

Jesse hesitated. Tim O'Mara matched his pause, seeming not to look at him, not to know he was there, tiny eyes appearing to watch everything within the mountain arena except his opponent. It was a bad trick, this thing of a man not looking at you when you were trying to get in on him. You couldn't see his eyes. And when you couldn't see a man's eyes you couldn't read his body. Jesse curved, wavered, took a half-step backward, finding himself confused, uncertain. And for the first time in his life, *afraid*.

As the mountain man's retreating foot felt behind him for a safe and solid setting he was necessarily, for the least fraction of split time, off balance. Tim struck instantly.

Whirling to roll with the lunge, Jesse's pivot foot struck a loose, fist-sized boulder. He felt the searing pain of the ankle-turn as the leg spun on out from under him, knew he was falling even before Tim's huge weight bombarded into him.

Where it should have cost him his life, the awkward fall saved it. Tim's leap, thrown off-time by his adversary's collapse, carried the burly Mormon's body on over its intended target, causing the thick grasp of the circling arms to miss their intended bearhug-close, instead, on the mountain man's desperately upflung arms. The next instant Jesse's drawn-up thighs had straightened, driving his bony knees up and into the twin pits of Tim's groins.

With the groin thrust, Jesse balled his body, rolled sideways to his hands and knees as Tim, ten feet away, came scrambling to his feet. It was now the Mormon's turn to hesitate, slowed by the intense pain of the double blow in his groins. It was a hesitation that sent Jesse leaping toward him, big fists clubbed. But the first surge of that leap sent a hot knife of sickening weakness up the calf of the mountain man's left leg, bringing him to a staggering halt five feet from

107

the waiting renegade. Whitefaced, Jesse tested the foot, found where it would just bear his weight. And no more.

The fight was ten seconds old, unjoined as yet, and he was going into it with a sprained ankle!

As the injured Jesse halted his rush, Tim wheeled and came at him, his headlong attack indicating a sudden disregard of caution and maneuver.

The indication was only apparent.

The big Mormon was one of those occasional humans whose instincts to kill or be killed had survived ten thousand years of civilized veneering. He came down on Jesse now, as one wolf would on another, sensing the fact of the mountain man's distress without knowing its nature. Without knowing and without caring, his animal-sharp extrasensory perception telling him as accurately as any certain knowledge that he had wounded his foe and had him going down.

Jesse did what he could, and it was not enough.

As the charging renegade leapt in, he set himself back on his good right leg and drove his fist full into the snarling face. At the instant the blow was delivered, Tim tucked his chin for the classic frontier brawler's diving headbutt. Jesse's whitened knuckles smashed into the matted hair and iron-hard bone of the Mormon's skull-top, the wrenching shock of the collision spearing up his straightened forearm and bicep to explode with rocket-bursting force in the spasmed muscles of his shoulder. He felt the rupturing impact of the bull's-head bury itself in the pit of his belly and knew he was falling again.

He had no sensation of striking the ground, his next memory being the perfectly clear one of an hour's long interval during which he could not breathe or move. The same clear, helpless consciousness told him that Tim had him in an arm-locked bearhug and was crushing the literal life out of him.

His breath, reflexing from the solar plexus smash of Tim's head, came bursting back with its swift, familiar burgeoning of fresh strength. Twisting to free his arms so that he could get his hands into Tim's face, he found his numbed right arm would not respond, while his left was pinned by the double prison of his own and his opponent's weights. At the same time he found the Mormon's great hips and legs had his own long limbs hopelessly wedged beneath them.

With the cool dimness of coming unconsciousness spreading its grateful shade before him, he forced his mind to work and his eyes to see.

What they saw was an ear. A thick-lobed, protruding, dirt-crusted human ear. It was attached to a big round head that was buried, grunting and straining, against the giving crack of his upper ribs. That was undoubtedly Tim O'Mara's head and the ear was undoubtedly Tim O'Mara's ear. With all of consciousness and strength that remained to him, Jesse flashed his white teeth down and into that ear.

He felt the grating of the parting cartilage as his jaws clamped crazily home, sensed the spasmodic, wild recoil of Tim's whole body, heard the animal pain in his hoarse cry.

Then he was free. Standing clear. His feet under him once more. His mind and vision glass-clean.

Tim was waiting across from him, dull face contorted, hairy left paw just coming away from the side of his head. Tim brought the hand down. Stared at it, wonderingly. Jesse's eyes followed the Mormon's, seeing the hand and the bright blood.

For a long five seconds the two stood silently, feet wide-braced, breaths close held, the Mormon letting his eyes come slowly up from the bloody hand to lock and hold with Jesse's only after what seemed an eternity to the waiting mountain man.

Tim was muttering now, like an angry, crazed beast, and backing away from Jesse to begin the circle again. The guarded maneuver narrowed the mountain man's eye, quickened his thinking.

With the leg gone, Jesse knew he had one chance; to keep Tim from guessing he was crippled and to make the hulking Mormon come to him. Slowly he moved on in, white with the pain of the ankle, yet making himself walk on it. Tim fell back into his circle, moving and looking away from the mountain man. In Jesse's mind the plan was forming. It had worked once by accident. It might work twice by intent.

He feinted a quick step forward, taking the weight on his good leg. Tim spun with the feint and as he spun Jesse spun with him, half slipping to one knee. Tim took the bait, his diving leap coming with a rush and a grunt that dazed Jesse with its speed. But this time the mountain man was in under it, and he had his feet under him. He felt his shoulder drive into the crush of the Mormon's hairy belly, got his palms against the great chest in the same instant. Coming erect, he straightened his long arms, the knotting shoulder muscles

109

cracking with the sudden, snapping heave. Tim's huge body appeared to hang in mid-air for a full second, the arc of its pause a good seven feet from the rocky ground. Then it was in the rocks, flat-sprawled, the contact force of its falling seeming to jar the very earth under Jesse's running limp.

It was a fall that would have broken a strong man's spine, but Tim rolled away from it and found his feet before Jesse could get him. Stunned, bleeding, half blind from the rock dust and pine needles that matted his broad face, the Mormon came groping and muttering toward the crouching Jesse.

The awkwardness of that limping run toward the fallen Tim had cost the mountain man a precious advantage, but it had brought him something equally dear. The turned ankle was strengthening. Would take its share of the weight now. Felt stronger by the second. A man could work with his feet under him. Could set himself to use those club-hard hands and swinging shoulders.

And more. Now was the time to use them.

Tim's last clear memory was of seeing the grim white face across from him suddenly ease into a wide-mouthed trace of a grin. Then he was reaching for his man and storming him under. The face was gone and the grin with it. There was nothing there, then, and his ears were ringing and he was coughing with the blood that was bleeding back from his nose and into his throat.

Head swinging, eyes blurring, the Mormon renegade found his man again. Now he was only a gray shadow, without face or arms or legs. And he was moving against a flatness and an emptiness that was as gray as his shadow. But he was moving, and Tim could see that.

Jesse set himself once more as Tim came weaving in, sighted the bloody mouth and nose, swung his arm three inches below them for the blunt chin. Again a last-moment lurch of the dazed Mormon steered the blow away from the hanging jaw, landing it with a tearing sideslash across the right eye and cheekbone. Tim's body twisted to the force of the smash, falling past Jesse to land with a tooth-setting wrench on the left side and shoulder.

From some ageless, dim, atavistic well of primal instinct, Tim O'Mara drew the last bucket of brute will. Somehow, unbelievably, he got to his knees. And then, incredibly, to his feet.

Turning with the last thrusting lurch which brought him

up, the right side of his face swung around broadside to Jesse. The mountain man saw the dead white of the exposed bone beneath the damaged eye, the formless mass of the closing flesh above it.

He knew then that instant, inner wash of cold-sickness which is the brave man's psychic rebellion against destroying another equally brave thing—be it brute or human. And then the sickness was gone and he was moving in on the sightless, whimpering renegade. Moving in to do what he had to do. And meaning to do it with every ounce of merciful strength that was in him.

Stooping, his groping fingers closed around the jagged, melon-sized rock, his weary arm drawing back and up as he straightened. For a long, slow breath the rock hung poised above the featureless pulp that had once been a fellow creature's face, then fell from the nerveless fingers to roll and bounce harmlessly in front of the knee-braced Tim O'Mara.

Jesse was still standing over the slumped huddle of the Mormon's sagging body, his mind and jaw setting to fight down the sickness that was building in him again, when he heard it.

It was a deep voice. And pleasant. Not angry, *and not English.*

"*Woyuonihan!* The Red Fox is a fighter. We respect him!"

The affable growl of the speech broke in a chain of High Plain's monosyllables which mounded Jesse's spine with gooseflesh. A man would never need to turn to guess that orator's identity. Still, it went against the mountain breed to take lead in the back without at least a farewell wave at what was undoubtedly getting ready to sling it there.

Before he could move to face around, however, the voice was continuing its guttural, unhurried way.

"Now, wait, Fox. Just step back there, where you are. Only a little ways—"

Without hesitation, Jesse moved to obey, placing his moccasins carefully behind him for three slow, backward steps, knowing the dangerous shift of these red minds, not wanting to bring that coup shot any sooner than necessary. On the third step, the voice came again.

"That's enough, cousin. You were in the way of that crawling dog, there—" The laconic words were punctuated with a single, barking rifle shot. Jesse heard the slug slap into the heaving chest of the still-conscious Tim O'Mara, saw

111

the big renegade's hands go jerking toward the spreading stain beneath the left nipple, watched them claw and knot, briefly, before the thick body slid forward into the granite and lay still. In the following quiet, Jesse turned, taking care that the movement was slow and steady.

A man had to grant they looked beautiful standing over there in the throat of the creek gorge.

Back of them the red morning sun bounced and gleamed off the rifle barrels and lance blades, the nervous pattern of their hundred war ponies making a motley pied background for the eagle feathers and war grease that draped and splattered their bodies. A hundred yards in their foreground, thirty from Jesse, his great size dwarfing the piebald stud horse he rode, the beautifully proportioned bulk of Watonga sat black and stark against the climbing sun.

"*Hau*," said Jesse. "We meet at last." Bowing slightly, he touched the tips of his left fingers to his brow. "*Woyuonihan*."

"*Woyuonihan*," responded Watonga, the near-black mask of his face cracking in a grotesque grin. "*Hohahe*, Tokeya Sha is welcome. Watonga has waited long for this pleasure."

"Tokeya is a fool!" replied Jesse, feigning a self-disgust which wasn't half a tone from bitterly real.

"*Iho!* Don't say that," begged the huge chief, solicitously. "Even when you were a boy Long Chin told my father you would one day be a chief. And now, look. Every *Shacun* north of the Medicine Road knows of The Red Fox. Tokeya Sha is a *real* chief! *Wagh!*"

"A real *heyoka*," insisted Jesse, stalling the precious seconds as his glance reckoned the distance to Heyoka's hiding place against the number of pony lengths between him and Black Coyote. "Were he not such a witless one, how could he have come so blindly to smell at this putrid bait?" He indicated the silent Tim with a contemptuous, back-flung gesture of his thumb.

"Big Face was telling the truth. He did not know we came back here to catch you. He thought we had gone. He thought I left him here as a Courtesy Return to Tokeya. And so I did. *Oha!* Take him! Watonga gives him back to you. But do not say he lied. He didn't know we were hiding in Little Chief's Valley. Big Face didn't know that."

Jesse nodded, understanding that by "Little Chief" they meant Kit Carson. Cuss the luck! His hunch about looking up

Carson's Creek Gorge had been dead right. As he hesitated, thus, he saw the braves behind Watonga beginning to split and file around either side of the Flats to hem and circle him in solid. There was no move to harm him, no apparent hurry to surround him. The ponies just shuffled silently, easily, along the cedars' edges, their blank-faced riders sitting slack and dead-eyed, not seeming to even look at the trapped goddam guide.

In another moment, the southern file of warriors would be between him and Heyoka. If he were going to make any break, now was it.

Still he hung back, fearing the odds, undecided, confused, as near to being stampeded as he had ever been. Finally, it was a little thing which decided him. One of those strange, stray little thoughts which will flash through a man's mind at a time like that ... the thought of Ousta, the dark-faced squaw.

Fronted by a hundred of the hardest-cut prairie warriors ever to swing astride a spotted pony, the Sioux-reared mountain man found himself thinking about one female squaw! And what he was thinking was that once these red sons got him back to camp and to that wild, hawk-headed Ousta, there would be a sharp end to all this Courtesy Rules horseplay.

The Indian men were great for ceremony, always. Their women, never. With the squaws it was meat in the pot or a scalp on the drying rack, and the hell with the details of how it got there.

All right, then, he would go now.

He tensed his body for the leap that was going to start his spring for Heyoka. If he could get to the cat-fast gray mare, he would give these red devils a ride they could lie to their grandchildren about for the next ten generations.

The panther-scream war cry of the Minniconjou welled up in his throat, his legs straightening for the jump.

The leap never got started, the yell, never out. A flashing burst of pain exploded in the back of his head. The red sun behind Watonga shattered and flew into a thousand pieces. The amber morning light went black as the nether pole. ...

Ousta was still spraddled over the fallen body, raising her stone maul for another drive at the bright red head beneath her, when Black Coyote's heavy voice interrupted.

"*Hinhanka po*, that's enough!"

The chief's barking command stopped the final hammer

113

blow, left the squaw staring up at her mate, broad mouth writhing like a sow bear that had just had her snout cuffed out of the hot bowels of a yearling doe.

"That red scalp is a fine one." growled Watonga irritably. "Why get it all gummed-up with the brains?"

7. ROCKPILE MEADOW

WHEN Jesse came awake, he was tied to a torture stake, twenty feet from the entrance flap of Watonga's lodge.

This stake was a real *Can Wakan Sha*, a real Red Holy Pole. Fifteen feet high, dyed a brilliant scarlet with the juice of the *wica kanaska* berry, its vibrant color was no more evident than the forecast of the trapped mountain man's future contained in its raw pigment. All doubts a man might have had as to how the Arapaho intended handling him were pleasantly resolved.

They aimed to barbecue him, North Plains style.

Down-canyon, he could see the hanging ledge and rank fern dell of Portola Springs. Around him and Watonga's lodge was scattered the circle of ash-gray mushroom spots marking the early morning ceremonial fires made to induce the spirit of Uncle Pte to co-operate in the upcoming slaughter of his four-legged patrons up on the mesa.

The camp appeared deserted, the angle of the sun, square in Jesse's face, indicating about 10.0 a.m. He'd been *tela nun wela*, "dead yet alive," near onto four hours.

Testing the rawhide thongs, he was pleasured to learn two things: his limbs were sound, his blood moving good. His head ached but his eyesight and mind were clear enough.

There was a considerable trick to stringing a man up so he would keep for hours in good condition, yet have no chance in the Lord's back pasture of working himself loose. The Arapaho proved they were on to this trick by the way they had laced him to that Holy Pole. Beyond testing the job he made no effort to loosen it. No point wasting good strength. These butchers knew how to hang their hogs.

The fact they had strung him up so careful, leaving his leggin's on, putting him in a nice shade clump, let him know they didn't aim to sweat him like they had figured for Tim.

115

Nobody raised with the *Shacun* needed any more telling than that about their plans for him. The only time they took care to keep a prisoner good and alive was when they reckoned to take their sweet time getting him good and dead.

As to the precise manner of this prospect, the mountain man wasn't held long in question.

Ousta came barging out of the cedars, noisy as a wind whisper in young grass. Her arms were loaded with straight-grain cedar chunks. Seeing Jesse's eyes on her, she nodded, displaying that curious Indian quirk which brought them to accept a condemned enemy as highly privileged. "*Hau*, you have been walking the shadows. *Hohahe*, welcome back."

"*Ho ha*," replied Jesse, straightfaced. "Thank you. That is fine wood you have there. Hard and dry. The splinters will be excellent."

The big squaw nodded again, approving the *Wasicun's* good guessing. "Indeed, nothing like dry cedar for a real roasting."

"*Hau*, it burns slow and long. The meat gets done right, that way."

The squaw grunted an agreement to Jesse's statement, squatting down in front of the lodge, beginning the loving work of splitting the foot-long burning splinters off the seasoned cedar.

Jesse gave her a few minutes to get started then inquired, politely. "Where are all the men? Where is Watonga and the Little Chief?"

"All gone," growled the squaw. "All gone to hunt. There is a fine herd up on the High Grass. Gray Bear and Elk Runner found it there. Black Coyote took Ya Slo, his son, along that the boy might learn how a herd is properly approached."

And that, apparently, was the end of her conversational efforts for the day. To the mountain man's further inquiries, she was deaf as a limestone post, her only further contribution to the palaver being to finally come up off her haunches, move over to the captive trapper and belt him in the mouth with one of the iron-hard cedar chunks, the blow being accompanied with a soft-grunted request to "Shut up, now!"

Jesse licked his split lip, speculatively, spat his mouth clear of blood, and complied.

For a pleasant hour, then, he was entertained by his contemplative viewing of Watonga's wife at her ingenious best—displaying all the fascinating hand skill of the Plains Tribes. The fact that the Arapaho woman's prairie artcraft

116

was being devoted to fashioning the shapely little hardwood splinters which would, with nightfall, be illuminating various and tender portions of Jesse Callahan's swart skin was irrelevant.

The woman was an artist.

Along about noon, business improved. First off, Watonga came riding down the mesa trail followed by Johnny O'Mara on his stubby paint pony. Jesse had time to sing out as the youngster spotted him.

"Hi there, Johnny boy! Are you all right?"

The put-on cheerfulness missed its mark with the dirty-faced boy, his answer coming with childish direction right to the point. "Gosh all hemlocks, Jesse! Am I glad to see you! Say, golly! What have they got you tied up for? I'll bet they're going to torture you, Jesse. Gee I—"

Evidently, the Indians hadn't let the little cuss see him when they had brought him into camp after Ousta had snuck up behind him in the Flats and floored him with that damn maul. Jesse was about to reassure Johnny that he was not in any danger but before he could Ousta grabbed the boy off his pony and hustled him into the tipi. Inside the lodge, the mountain man could hear the squaw growling at him like a shebear warning her cub. Hearing nothing from Johnny, Jesse called out, still putting his words light and easy. "Don't you worry none, Johnny. They ain't going to harm me none. You watch, now. The Arapaho ain't been whelped what can handle us Minniconjou. *H'g'un*, in there, Wanbli Sha. Keep your heart big and your ears wide open!"

There was no answer from the tipi and shortly Ousta came out to join Watonga where the chief squatted by the lodge entrance. Looking at her mate frowningly, the squaw demanded, "What happened? Why did you return? Where are the braves?"

Black Coyote shrugged. "It was nothing. Such a thing as will happen no more. We got a bad change in wind and the buffalo smelled us. They began to run before we could get around them. Yellow Leg and the others went after them. I brought Ya Slo back, that's all."

"*Waste*, it is good you did. Ya Slo should sleep. Last night his eyes were wide open to the smokehole as long as the stars were there."

"*Hau*," rumbled Watonga, "mine, too. You can't sleep much around that damn Tokeya Sha. I haven't had my eyes closed right since he fooled me about that gunpowder. Right

117

now, I am tired. Like an old chief with six young wives. Curse that red-haired *Wasicun* devil. Curse his red-wheeled goddam. Curse that gunpowder—!"

"Not the powder!" Ousta said, quickly. "Don't curse the powder. Don't put a bad dream on that. Remember, we must get powder soon. Don't curse it, then!"

The chief scowled the squaw down, snapped at her irascibly. "That red-wheeled goddam is the curse of my life. It has defeated me. It is a devil. An evil thing. I would give much to have it in my hands. *Wagh!* At least I have the *Wasicun* who guided it against me. Who ruined my honor agreement with the Mormon chief. Now, we'll see. I'll kill him. Maybe that will count as a coup against the goddam. Do you think so?"

"Oh, sure. But sleep, now. Don't think about it. Old Horse has dreamed that you will get the powder. Maybe the Mormon chief means to give it to you after he has captured Big Throat's fort. Anyway, Old Horse always dreams right. You will get that powder. And soon."

Observing this conversation, Jesse was aware of Johnny O'Mara's pinched face peering out from under the lodge's sideskins, a few feet from the entrance flap. The boy looked about as drowsy as a tom kitten in an Airedale kennel. He caught the mountain man's eye at once, waved quickly, disappeared back under the sideskins. Another second and his high voice was piping defiant disregard of Ousta's warning to be quiet.

"Don't worry, Jesse. We'll get away all right!"

The mountain man had no more than winced helplessly at this boyish optimism, than Johnny's voice concluded with a bull's-eye shout that hit dead center of Jesse's bitter sunsquint.

"Shucks, we've still got our Sioux secret, ain't we?"

As the meaning of the boy's words struck into Jesse's thoughts, the big Arapaho squaw was inside the lodge, scolding the youngster angrily, cutting his words sharp off. But the mountain man had heard all he needed. And a heap more than he had expected or hoped for.

Maybe it wasn't much, but a hid-out Green River skinning knife was for sure a sight more of a something than the nothings Jesse had been able to think of for the past two hours. As this hope arose in the mountain man, Ousta came out of the lodge, standing aside for Black Coyote to enter.

118

"What have you done with Ya Slo, inside there?" the chief demanded.

"He is quiet, tied by the leg to a lodgepole."

"*Waste*," replied her mate. "Now we will sleep. The hunters will be returning by the time Old Father Wi* has traveled almost to the west. See that you have plenty of burning splinters by then, woman. I owe this Minniconjou Fox a real roasting."

"There will be plenty. I will make more while Watonga sleeps."

Jesse figured that Black Coyote, like any seasoned soldier, would not need more than five minutes to be asleep. He gave him ten, then began anxiously hawk-eyeing the sideskins of his lodge where he'd last seen Johnny O'Mara's gopher face.

Another endless five minutes crawled by and the sideskins hadn't even quivered. Well, it had been a long shot, last chance, at best. Even if the gutty cub had meant that he still had the knife Jesse'd given him, he would never get the chance to use it with that outsize squaw squatting there splitting those cussed splinters.

The mountain man's slant gaze swung away from the lodge, narrowed down on the busy squaw. She looked up, catching his eye, nodded grimly, held up one of the splinters for his approval. He nodded, politely, and she fell again, loose-smiling, to the loving concentration required by her labors. The second her glance left him, Jesse caught an eye-tail of light from the direction of the lodge.

Then he was looking at the three brightest spots an Arapaho-bound white man ever saw under the slight-raised sideskins of a hostile *Shacun* lodge: the lively sparkle of two Johnny O'Mara-blue eyes, and the sun-bounce off the glittering blade of a Green River knife.

Now, by cripes! If that horse-size squaw would somehow turn her back for twenty breaths. Man Above! Wakan Tanka! Make her do it. Send her down something to do besides sitting there hacking away at those lousy burning splinters!

The next second's reaction on Ousta nearly made an Indian Christian out of Jesse Callahan.

As though in ordered obedience to the mountain man's

---

* The sun, patron deity of all the Plains Tribes.

fervent prayer, the Arapaho woman suddenly stood up. Glancing at the prisoner, she scowled, went limping off into the brush.

Good old Wakan Tanka! Bless that Man Above!

The next instant Jesse's warning sidemouth hiss was on its way toward the sleeping chief's lodge. And Johnny O'Mara was popping out from under the sideskins, leaping across the open, racing wide-eyed down upon the waiting mountain man.

"The hands first, boy! For the luvva Pete, slash them thongs. Never mind if you get a little meat along with them!"

He felt the bite of the razored blade whacking the rawhide laces, felt them loosen and fall slack. Writhing, he seized the knife from the white-faced boy, low-voiced his tense order.

"Back in the lodge, young un! Hop it before she sees you!"

Without waiting to see his harsh command obeyed, Jesse bent forward, slashing at the intricate knottings of the ankle rawhides. Another second, now. Just one. Looking up to check the squaw, his fingers frantically seeking out the twistings of the thongs, the better to get the knife at them, he was in time to see Ousta coming for him.

Passing the splinter pile, the long arm swept down, scooping up the stone maul. Three more big-cat leaps and she was on him, the grating grizzly coughs of her people coming with her.

Jesse measured her diving drive, twisted as far left as his bound feet would let him. The stone maul missing, hissing by his ear an arrow's width away. As it passed, Jesse shifted the knife to his left hand, his right striking, snake-like, for the squaw's right wrist. Striking and going home. Nailing the squaw's arm clean as a ten-penny spike. At the same instant, he put every ounce of the power in his tendon-tough muscles into a wrenching shoulder twist.

He felt the Indian woman's wrist bones turn and snap under his fingers, saw the falling stone maul leave the squaw's nerveless fingers. Simultaneously, his free left hand whipped the skinning knife into her contorted back.

White mountain man, stone buffalo maul and knifed Arapaho squaw all hit the ground together, Jesse's clawing right hand biting into the maul's haft as he did. Ousta flung herself to one side, surging to free her broken right wrist from the *Wasicun's* grip, found that the hand brought up in the iron school of Minniconjou horse-breaking doesn't give worth a puny damn. The squaw had time to start one last broken growl, and that was all.

With everything he had to offer, from his memories of little Kathy's crushed face onward, Jesse drove the stone maul square into the snarling face. The pop and splatter of the pulping bones, the way the maul broke in past the nose bridge, sudden-soft and deep, let him know that Ousta, The Limper, the wife of Watonga, had split her last burning splinter.

Twisting free of the squaw's body, Jesse came away from it as Black Coyote stumbled to the opening of the lodge. The chief's eyes, heavy with sleep, sized the situation a little slowly. When it came to him that the *Wasicun* was cutting himself free, Watonga wasted no breath in warwhooping. Crouching for his leap at the still tethered white man, his knife flashed into his hand.

Jesse needed five seconds more. Got them by grace of Johnny O'Mara's quick-headed thinking.

As Watonga launched himself through the tipi flap, his own four-foot coupstick banged itself between his bowed legs, knocking him as head over heels as a bear cub in a scuffle-play. Before he could come clear of the ground, Jesse was on him.

Black Coyote got as far as his knees when the mountain man's size eleven stomper took him dead in the stomach pit. The bursting pain of the groin kick doubled the chief forward into the split-oak fist that followed the foot. Watonga jackknifed down into the dirt, his great jaw sagging. He rolled half over on his back, lay there glaze-eyed as a pole axed steer.

"We got plenty of time," Jesse's reassuring nod went to Johnny O'Mara, where the nervous youth sat his paint pony fifty yards downtrail of Watonga's buffalo camp. "Just you set there and hold on to Heyoka and the studhoss of the chief's. I'm going back to the camp a minute. I got a message I want to pin on old Watonga."

He was gone, loping easily back toward the silent Indian camp, before Johnny could put his nerves into words. White-faced, the boy sat his pony, dividing his frightened glances between keeping an eye out for Jesse's return, and seeing to the considerable business of holding onto Watonga's skittery piebald stallion. Heyoka, the mountain man's indispensable but immoral mare, did her bit to heighten Johnny's trial by choosing to make the most of this, her first opportunity in months, to be alone with a gentleman. The way she kept sidling up to the nostril-belled attentions of Black Coyote's best buffalo horse, along with that animal's earnest, if ungallant, efforts to shove his muzzle under her flirtatious, outstretched neck, were like to pull the boy's thin arms clean off.

Breaking out his manliest seven-year-old oath, the near-panicked youth belted the watch-eyed stud frantically across the nose. "Dang your mangy 'Rapaho hide! Leave that there mare alone! Jesse'll kill the both of us, happen you bust loose of me—!" Whether annoyed by Heyoka's delicate Minniconjou scent, or impressed by the plain audacity of a weanling *Wasicun* boy's gall in rope-swatting a chief's war mount, the ear-pinned stud backed off, cleared his offended nostrils disdainfully, and quieted down.

Johnny, cinching down the grip of his stubby fingers on the two lead ropes and the bite of his best buck teeth on his quivering lower lip, swung his pinched face again toward the uptrail bend where Jesse had disappeared.

With true Sioux sense of the properly dramatic, the mountain man had, before leaving the camp with Johnny, strung the unconscious Watonga up on the Holy Pole from which he himself had just escaped. His only addition to the rawhide embroidery the hostiles had sewed him up with had been to clamp a snug Arapaho halter on the helpless chief.

Now, returning happily to the haltered coyote, he had his message to leave with him. And he hadn't been keen on Lacey's boy seeing him deliver the little token of fond farewell, either.

And for very quickly evident cause.

The fact that Watonga had recovered consciousness when Jesse got back to him didn't dampen the mountain man's fine red enthusiasm one morsel. Whipping out Ousta's gutting knife, he took the awkward weapon by the back of the blade, holding it like a skin-painting stick. As the chief's expressionless eyes followed him, he brushed the flies off the sun-black chest and went carefully to carving his parting Minniconjou pictograph thereon.

Jesse was no artist by the exacting Plains Indians standards, but when he had finished his tongue-screwed labors on Watonga's bust, the incisions hurriedly rubbed with a little salt and trade tobacco from the chief's own pouches, he had a readably good design.

Any Plains Tribe cub of eight or ten could have told you it

was an unmistakable Minniconjou Fox, leg-hoisted and leaving sign upon an equally undeniable Arapaho coyote.

Jesse broke around the trailhead in a reaching dogtrot, loped up to the tearfully grateful Johnny O'Mara, and grabbed the halter rope of Watonga's stud as the boy flung it hastily to him. Swinging up on the crouching stallion, he immediately balled one horny fist and drove it down between the nervous brute's ears with a force that like to knocked the ugly jughead off the scrawny neck. Watonga's war horse established a record for losing all interest in the opposite sex and completely forgetting his own, left off his nervous crouching and went to standing as broke and gentle as a second-string travois pony.

With his borrowed charger properly chastised, the mountain man turned his attention to the waiting Johnny O'Mara.

"All quiet in the Land of the Coyote!" He grinned broadly, cocking his head back toward the Indian camp and fetching his small redheaded companion a reassuring bearpaw thump on the shoulder. "I don't like to crow, boy, but when your Uncle Jesse quietens them down, they stay silent-like! You ain't going to hear no more Injun peeps today."

The brag was no sooner out than it tripped headlong on its own boast.

From up on the mesa trail, no more than half a mile above Watonga's black lodge, it came. Long, low, weirdly beautiful: the hunting song of the buffalo wolf.

"Son of a she-dog!" the curse snapped off Jesse's tongue like a shot bowstring. "Me and my big mouth."

"What's the matter, Jesse? What *was* that?"

"Scout signal," grunted the mountain man.

"Gee, it sounded more like a loafer howling, huh, Jesse?"

"Well, it was a kind of loafer, boy. Like none you ever seed, I allow." His companion's agreement came acidly. "That loafer up there is near six foot tall, carries a smooth red coat with a sprouting of long eagle feathers around the skull."

"You mean Injuns, Jesse?"

"I don't mean field mice, young un. Shut up. You'll hear quick enough."

On top of his gruff order, Jesse threw his head back and howled dismally in reply to the Arapaho signal. The call had just time to echo up under the mesa rim before it was seized up and flung back from above, attended this time by a whole discordant symphony of assorted wolf howls.

"Gosh! It *is* Injuns—"

"You got it figured, boy. Come on, toss me Heyoka's lead rope. And get yourself set solid on that scrub paint. Them's Black Coyote's boys. They're back from the hunt somewhat sooner than I allowed. About six hours 'somewhat' I'd say. *Aii-eee*, Johnny boy! We got us some big bottom-pounding to do, now."

With all three horses hitting a flat gallop, Jesse set himself to figure a little Arapaho algebra. Well, one thing was easy, even before you started sweating. There wasn't any question of what trail to take. The first five miles back to Cedar Flats was as laid-out and one-way as a fairground racetrack.

But that wasn't getting your figuring done. After Cedar Flats, it was another ten miles to Rockpile Meadow, and then another ten miles to the Medicine Road. If you ever got that far you had a chance of running into some white pack outfit working between Fort Bridger and Laramie. That, or maybe Andy Hobbs and the skinners coming up from Old Gabe's. The last chance was about as fat as a she-grizzly coming out of her winter sleep sucking six early cubs. But fat or lean, ribby or raunchy, just about your best chance at that.

There could be no doubling back, no laying hid-up to let the hostiles run by you. The canyon, all the way out, was that narrow a trade rat couldn't have stuck his big toe out from one side of it without some trailing Arapaho would stomp on it going by.

Second place, there was no cut-off along the way. The only opening in the hundred-foot canyon walls in the entire twenty-five miles was the mouth of Carson's Creek Gorge at Cedar Flats. And as far as Jesse knew, that ran into a blind box three miles from the Flats.

It came square down to a stretch-out race, with the odds a hundred-to-two against him and the kid reaching the Medicine Road.

The biggest hitch was their horses.

The mountain man had planned to rope a string of the best ponies out of the big Indian herd at the camp, lead and ride them in relays, thus giving him and the boy fresh, fast mounts the whole way into Fort Bridger. The unexpected return of the buffalo hunters had gutted that clean. They'd had to cut and run with only Johnny's short-legged paint, Watonga's spooky studhorse and good gray Heyoka.

124

On the studhorse he had slung two parfleches, one loaded with the pick of Black Coyote's possibles: a few pounds of jerked buffalo beef, a couple of pints of good powder, fifty galena pills (plus, hastily slung across the boy's saddle horn, Watonga's fancy old Hawken rifle); the other parfleche he had crammed with something his Indian eye had spotted in the chief's lodge and which his Sioux soul hadn't been able to resist—fifty pairs of beautiful worked Arapaho moccasins, the net proceeds of The Limper's long summer evenings, lovingly packed for the winter trade at Deseret.

In the optimism of fresh horses and a six-hour start, Jesse had allowed he might as well turn that profit as not. Arapaho moccasins were the best on the plains, went whizzing at three dollars a brace anywheres a mountain man could get his paws on a pair. Too much the born trader, Jesse Callahan, to turn down a hundred-and-fifty-dollar gain for two minutes of extra packing. Not when he and Lacey and the boy would need every cent they could get to set up in California, anyways.

Now, with equal decision and eye for the future, the mountain man went out of the moccasin business.

Slowing the galloping stallion, he seized the near parfleche, slashing the rawhide cross strap through. The next second Johnny's pony and the trailing Heyoka were bucking through a hundred-and-fifty-dollar shower of handmade Arapaho footskins, and Jesse was grimly lacing the remaining parfleche hard and flat and fast to his saddle horm.

Right now, the going price of two pints of powder and fifty rifle balls was higher than a fortful of fancy Indian footgear.

Looking back to check how Johnny had survived the moccasin spattering, the mountain man handed himself the luxury of a short grin. The half-pint sprout was all right. Grinning right back at him there. Quirting his little pony along, busy as a monkey on a dog's back. And withal hanging on to the cumbersome, four-foot barrel of Watonga's elegant Hawken as though his life depended on it—which it sure as thunder might, come another five miles.

Jesse patted the worn buttwood of Old Sidewinder, his own treasured Hawken, hurriedly recovered among the plunder in the chief's lodge. Mister, if he went under, he'd take a few along with him. Given the boy to pour and prime, with two top guns to handle, he'd make the red sons come. Happen he could find the right spot to hole up when the time came, he'd throw a good part of them for keeps.

This comforting plant had put down about half its first tender root in Jesse's mind when it curled up and died aborning.

Backtrail, a scant two miles, a yammer of Arapaho wolf howls blossomed high and sudden. Yellow Leg and the buffalo hunters had come home. Hearing the Indian howls, Johnny belabored his pony up even with Watonga's scrubby stallion. "Hey, Jesse! Here they come, huh? That's them, ain't it?"

"That's them, boy. But they ain't coming just yet. Kick the stuffing out'n that pony, Johnny. We can win another mile, maybe two, before they cut the chief down and get lined out after us. They been running buffer and they'll have to catch up and change horses. That'll take five minutes. Ride, boy. You ain't even trying. Whang your pony across the bottom with that gunstock. He'll go if you larrup him. Hang on—!"

With the shout, Jesse demonstrated his instructions by belting the boy's pony across the rump with his own Hawken's butt. The little paint squalled and jumped, churning his short legs. Johnny hung on and kept up the belting.

For the next two miles they ate big trail. Then the runt pony began to fade. Come the open of Cedar Flats, he was done. The mountain man, figuring they had four miles on the hostiles, shouted to Johnny to pull up in mid-clearing. As the boy did so, Jesse ran Heyoka up alongside the blowing pony. "Pile over on Heyoka, boy. Hang on to that rifle. That's the idea. You all set?"

"Sure. Where we going now, Jesse?"

"Never you mind," the mountain man slapped the studhorse with his rifle, "you jest burr on to that saddle horn and leave the mare to take her own way. She'll follow me as long as there's a jump left in her."

In the next fifteen minutes they made three of the ten miles to Rockpile Meadow, were topping out on Spanish Saddle. This crossbridge, the only considerable rise in the floor of Carson's Canyon, gave the lone view of the backtrail offered in the full length of the defile. From it, Jesse could look back and down on the distant clearing of Cedar Flats.

He kicked Watonga's stud on over the crest of the ridge, haunchslid him to a stop on the far side. Waving back to Johnny, he sang out, "Hi there, boy. Get that mare down off'n the skyline. Hurry on!"

As Johnny brought the mare sliding down the trail, Jesse caught her cheekstrap to keep her from plunging on down the roof-steep decline. "Here, young un. Set tight on the mare and clutch this stud's lead rope. Keep it short. Don't let him get to smelling around Heyoka. She's apt to nip him good and likely belt his ribs in too. And we ain't in no place to be putting on no two-hoss courtship on this here six-foot ledge. You get the idee?"

The boy peered over the trail edge at the thin stream of Carson's Creek eighty feet below, gulped, tried a laugh that came out a gargle, reassured the mountain man. "Yeah, sure, Jesse. All right. Where you going, now?"

"Back up on the ridge and take a belly flop. You know. So's I can see the Injuns crossing Cedar Flats. Our hosses have got to have a blow, too. They can take it right here as good as the next place. This way we'll get them a breather and give me a chance to see how far back the hostiles are. We can't see them again short of Medicine Road. Hold them hosses now, boy!"

Slipping around the panting mounts, the mountain man backhanded the gray mare a sharp crack on her sooty nose. "Stay, Heyoka! You move a muscle toward that stud, I'll hamstring you clean up to your croup."

Seconds later, the red-haired trapper was bellying up on the ridge and squinting over its granite spine. And a half-breath after that he was popping his eyes bigger than sour-dough flapjacks.

He had figured to have close to fifteen minutes for the horses to blow before the pursuing Arapaho would hit Cedar Flats—found he had the shagtail end of *one*. And he used part of that rolling down off the ridge to leg it for Johnny and the horses. Cripes! The last of the red buzzards had been slamming, hell-for-yellow-leather, across the clearing before he'd gotten his eyes over the lip of the ridge, and had disappeared in a cloud of red dust and distance-thin wolf yammers before he could get his sight properly squinted.

"Last one away's a hindtit pig!" he yelled at Johnny, crawling aboard Watonga's startled stud with the yell. "Hit the trail, boy. We're back in business!"

Johnny hadn't time to do anything but hold on. Heyoka was off down the narrow trail pellmell as a redbone hound with a razorback sow in tow. They rode now with nothing but the exploding grunts and paunchwater belly sounds of the straining horses making the conversation.

In two miles, with five yet to go to Rockpile Meadow, Watonga's stallion began to go under. Jesse felt the mean flutter of the big heart under the gaunt ribs, sensed the rhythm of the gallop going rough under him. Punctuating the discovery, a fresh burst of Arapaho howling broke out back-trail.

Aii-eee! If those redbirds hadn't made up near a mile on him and Johnny, he'd kiss a blue-nosed buffalo!

Heyoka, snorting and chopping foam at the stud's rump, was still going smooth as a hawk downwind. God bless the mud-ugly devil. She was only getting to her bottom when two ordinary horses had already run clear through theirs.

"Johnny!" his backflung shout brought an answering wave from the boy, "leave the mare come up alongside me when we hit the open ground yonder!"

With the command, the mountain man pulled the stud aside, letting the boy shoot Heyoka forward. "Ease out'n the saddle, there!" he shouted, gesturing abruptly. "No, no! Not up on her withers, boy! Back on the cantle. Cuss it all, get back there out'n the way. Make room. I'm coming aboard with you!"

With the two horses running shoulder-to-shoulder, Jesse bellowed at the mare. "*Hee-yahh!* Heyoka! *Waste, waste.* Bear in, gal. *In,* you muddy vixen! Shoulder in. C'mon here—" The mare, eyes rolling, ears plastered flatter than a beargrease haircut, crowded over into the faltering stallion. Jesse flung his off leg clear, letting her come in. The next second he was aboard her, bowed legs clamping her heaving barrel, lean arms snaking along her lathered neck to grab the loose-flying reins.

"Grab yourself a hold of that knifebelt of mine, young un. Here we go. *Hii-yee-hahh!*" The Minniconjou war cry echoed shrilly in the narrow canyon, putting another foot to the gray mare's reaching stride.

A mile. Four left, now. Three miles. Two left. Still she ran. Not so smooth, now. Rough, now. Ragged-rough. Lungs sobbing. Heart in spasm. Flared nostrils belling red as fresh blood. The hollow roar of windbreak building in the coughing gulps of air.

A mile, then. One more mile. A mile to Rockpile Meadow. *Rockpile Meadow?*

What was Rockpile Meadow? Just a name for a pile of horse-high boulders in the middle of a quarter-mile grassflat. Why, then, did it keep repeating itself in a man's mind as he
128

rode the last jumps out of a dying horse? Rode with a weanling redhead kid pounding the cantle behind him. Then, even as they went that last mile, the hostile wolf howls crawling up their rumps, two jumps for every one they were making, Jesse knew why. Knew why Rockpile Meadow had been hammering at his memory.

His plan shaped, now, as they ran. Shaped to the breaking stagger of Heyoka's splaying feet. Shaped to that last-gasp name—*Rockpile Meadow*.

By cripes, if he could make it into those boulders, he would carve that meadow name on a few Arapaho hides for keeps. He'd make them remember Rockpile Meadow! He would if he and the boy could make it there.

And they made it.

What difference that Heyoka went to her knees a hundred yards out? Sent them sprawling, hard and headlong? Other men had run for other rocks off the buckled backs of down horses. The main thing was, they made it. Made it with time for Jesse to kick the slobbering mare to her feet, handlead her in a weaving trot on into the boulder pile. Made it with time to slash the ammunition parfleche off the saddle, load and prime the two rifles while barking out the steps in the process for Johnny to watch and get the hang of.

Three minutes after they slid into the rocks the mountain man had Old Sidewinder poured, patched, rammed and shouldered, its ugly brown snout leveled through a chin-high crevice in the rockfringe fronting the backtrail entrance into the meadow.

And three and a half minutes after they slid in, the Arapaho bombarded out of the trail mouth and into the open meadow.

In their van, knifecut blood still lacing his black chest in bright red filigree, Watonga stood in his stirrups, cursing his second choice, blue roan war horse, frantically howling his followers on.

Jesse shoulder-nudged Old Sidewinder's stock, shifting its thick muzzle three inches to the right, bringing the V-notch of the rear sight across the distant ripple of Black Coyote's belly muscles. Three hundred yards. *H'g'un.* Two hundred and fifty. *Hunhunhe.* Let them come on. Get it down to two hundred. *Hii-eee!* Now!

Finger squeezing off, both eyes open like any sharp shot's ought to be, Jesse suddenly hunched the rifle muzzle another two inches to the right, swerving the V-notch off Watonga's belly, filling it with the shorter Dog Head's throatbase. With the recoil punching his jaw, the mountain man wondered why he'd done it. Why he'd pulled off his head on the chief, put it on the hapless Dog Head.

The shot seemed to roll out slower than the subchief's answering scream. Jesse saw the red hands fly to the throat and then there was open meadow in the sight's V-notch. Dog Head, fourth-line chief among the lodges of Watonga, was on his way to *Wanagi Yata*, his one-way lead ticket punched square and true through the Adam's apple.

With the blast of the hidden rifle and Dog Head's flopping dive, the following Indians checked their ponies hard up, their followers in turn banging into them, piling the whole forepart of the pack into a confused tangle. Only a handful of the front runners had marked the flash of Jesse's gun, the bulk of them not yet guessing the source of the subchief's ambush.

Jesse didn't keep them long in doubt.

"Gimme that gun, boy. Load this un. And see you take your time and do it right."

Grabbing Watonga's Hawken from the gaping youngster, he scuttled forty feet to the right, snapped an offhand shot into the maw of the milling pack. Two ponies reared, screaming, showing him he'd gotten a lucky one in, drilling the first horse to tap the second.

By now, the Arapaho had counted two separate flashes, were beginning to break back for the meadow's edge, undecided.

The mountain man raced back past Johnny, snatching back his own Hawken as the boy finished pouring the powder. Diving behind a big boulder thirty feet to the left of his original shot, he spat the spare galena pill from his mouth into the muzzle, banging the stock on the ground to seat the charge, not having time to ram it home with the hickory wiping stick. For sure, it wouldn't do much damage when it got out there, but it would get *out there*. Right now the idea wasn't a center shot. It was just any old shot.

Blam! The third shot whanged across the open, taking Elk Runner's bay mare fair under her flag, sending her pitching and squalling like she'd had a hayfork rammed into her.

That did it. *Hopo*, get out! *Hookahey*, back to the timber! *Wagh!* Where had the reinforcements come from? Who was out there in those rocks with Tokeya Sha and Ya Slo? Two shots, well, maybe the boy was shooting. But three? Who would know? *A-ah*, now was the time to look out. Something wrong here.

Back at the meadow edge, the hostiles powwowed, millingly. Shortly, two groups began skirting the edge of the open grass, keeping back of the timber, one group each way around the meadow. They traveled slowly, eyes intent on the ground.

Watching from the rockpile, Jesse spoke thoughtfully to Johnny O'Mara. "They're tracking us out, young un. Aiming to see did we get out'n the meadow, or did somebody else get into it."

"Gee, what'll they do then, Jesse? Reckon they'll sculp us?"

"Not you, boy. You'll make out, happen I work it right. They'll come for us right sudden now, though. When they meet up over there on the far side, they'll know it's just us and nobody else out there. Then we'll catch it, sure as Old Sidewinder shoots high and left."

"Say, looks to me like your piece held plumb center, Jesse. You sure nailed that old Dog Head right in the neck." Johnny was more impressed at the moment with the marksmanship of one white Minniconjou than with the threat of a hundred red Arapaho.

"It don't though, boy. That's why I got it named Old Sidewinder. Strikes like a crotchety buzztail. Hits on the upgo and a trifle left of center."

"It sure hits for you! High, left or anyways."

"They'll hit where you hold them, young un. Happen you know where to hold them. You—"

"Hey, look!" the excited youngster interrupted. "They're staying over there. Look at them waving their arms around!"

"Shut up," snapped the mountain man. "Leave me read them signs."

For three minutes the Arapaho talked back and forth over the heads of Jesse and Johnny, signaling with broad hand gestures and a series of barks and howling cries that sounded like nothing nearer than a loafer pack bickering over a division of buffalo guts.

As they conversed across the quarter-mile bowl of grassland, Jesse translated for his big-eyed companion. He didn't call the signal barks like he was talking to a seven-year-old, either. When a man reckons he's run his kite string down to the winding stick, he talks. Happen he's one of two

131

whites betwixt a hundred red Indians, he does. And birthdays don't mean a mortal thing. It's blood talking to blood and the cleanest way to say it is to say it short.

Leastways, if you mean it to be that you're saying goodbye.

"That's Elk Runner over there, Johnny, and Gray Bear with him. I think that's Blood Face doing the signal-calling. Apparently he's their head tracker. He's telling Watonga that no tracks come out'n the meadow over there. Now he's waving that there ain't one coming in neither. There he goes saying it must be only Tokeya Sha and Ya Slo out here in the rocks. That's it, boy."

The mountain man flicked his eyes to Watonga's group. "Now, you watch old Black Coyote. He'll give them their marching orders. This is where we come in. There he goes, see?"

The boy nodded, wide eyes pinned on the gracefully gesturing chief. "What's he telling them, Jesse? What's old Black Coyote saying to do?"

Jesse, watching the chief, tensed suddenly. Ignoring the boy's questions, he reached one long arm over to draw Johnny close to him. His voice was low, with no shred of excitement in it, but the narrowed eyes behind it burned fever-bright.

"Boy, listen to me. They've caught up to old Jesse. They're going to rush us. Both sides against the middle. Now, get this"—the mountain man pointed the flat lie with serious fingerwags—"I can tell by their signs that they aim to take us alive. But when they bust into these rocks, a-hossback, a little shaver like you might get stomped on, accidental-like. So here's how you play it. When they start for us, you head out'n them rocks to the north, there. Right through that opening. You mark the one I'm pointing?"

"Yes, sir. Gosh, Jesse, you mean you want me to run out there as soon as they come at us?"

"And keep running," the mountain man spoke sharply. "Scoot like a cottontail bunny with his flag on fire."

"What are you going to do?" The youngster eyed his companion, suspiciously. "Stay here?"

"I'll be right behind you," Jesse assured him. "That'll give them a chance to come up on us in the open. Nobody'll get trompled, see?"

"Why'nt we just surrender now?" The boy's direct question

132

jolted Jesse's yarn, forced him to throw a thickening handful of pure slop into the thin soup he was ladling up.

"Listen, boy. They'd figure it for a trick and ride right into us. This way they'll know we're giving in, straight. You do as I say and you'll see I'm right."

"Gee, I dunno. I—"

"Just do it, goldang you, boy. Don't argue."

"All right, Jesse. I guess you know—"

"You just betcha. So long, boy." The mountain man wrapped the youngster in a bear hug that popped his trusting blue eyes. "You mark what Old Jesse said. Run like blue fire when they start in for us. Don't look back at me. You might stumble and get yourself tromped after all. Now, get over in them north rocks. Keep your eye on me and when I wave, you scoot!"

Johnny scuttled over into the far rocks, crouched, trembling fearfully, awaiting the mountain man's go-sign.

Jesse hoped he had figured it halfway sound.

You could never tell about those flighty red devils, though. That was the trouble. However, if the kid had any chance, it was to get out in the clear as far away from Jesse Callahan as he could leg it. Watonga had Tokeya Sha where his hair was shorter than a scalded hog's. And the big black-skinned chief had blood in his small slant eye—Minniconjou blood.

Happen the boy got in the way of the Arapaho head-men getting to that blood, he'd get hurt. Out in the open and running away, chances were near sure some buck would make a dead gallop catch-up of him, and lug him clear of the fracas. *Wagh!* There'd be plenty of honor in that. Grabbing Watonga's foster son right out from under the *Wasicun's* magic Holy Iron. Scooping Ya Slo, unharmed, from under the very muzzle of Tokeya the Minniconjou's *mazawakan*. *Wagh*, indeed!

Anyways, that was as close as a man could set it up for the boy. Johnny might make it, might not. He'd have his chance. *Nohetto.* A man did what he could, then let it lay.

Shrugging, the mountain man turned his rifle-eye on his own prospects.

Half a look was plenty. The Arapaho, both sides of the meadow, were ready. On the up-canyon side, Watonga was wheeling his roan gelding in front of the main force. Twenty yards down the waiting line, Yellow Leg pivoted his pony in imitation of the chief's revolving horsemanship. Across-meadow, the thirty braves with Blood Face stood hooking their toes in their ponies' surcingles, hawk-eyeing the gyrations of their chief and Yellow Leg.

In his rockpile, Jesse watched the weaving turns of the ponies with equal interest, if inferior anticipation. The Sioux-taught mountain man understood the pattern and purpose of that maneuver as well as any Arapaho within rifleshot.

Watonga and Yellow Leg were riding the *Icapsinpsincela*, The Swallow, the circling signal ride that announced the preliminaries were done—the final act coming onstage. When the tracks of their ponies crisscrossed, lookout. When the hoofprints came together and divided like the forked tail of the wheeling swallow, *A-ah!* That was the time.

And the time was now.

Watonga spun his blue roan hard left, heeling him straight for Yellow Leg's mount. The subchief hauled his pony around to meet the approach of his chief. The two careening horses veered at the last moment, crossing each other in the lethal forked angle.

The scaling red granite float of the meadow floor churned to the hammer of four hundred barefoot pony hoofs. Jesse whirled, flagging Johnny to run. The boy caught the signal, started to run, got out in the clear past the rocks, got his first look at the lance-streaming Indian Charge.

Skidding to a stop, his childish cry wobbled back to the mountain man. "Come on, Jesse! Oh gosh, look at them come!"

"Go on, boy!" Cuss the little devil's redhead hide. "Run, cuss you Johnny, run!"

Johnny O'Mara hesitated half a second, turned and ran. Ran like old Jesse had told him. Scooting like a single-tail bunny. Straight back toward the mountain man.

Jesse threw his left arm wide, hooking the sliding youngster to his side, cursing him while he hugged him, winking the first tear he could ever remember out of his ice-blue eye, snarling at him like he'd heard Ousta snarling at him in that tipi, and thinking for the first time how the giant squaw must have felt about this freckleface tadpole. "Dadburn you, boy! I'll flay your bottom raw for you. I told you to run. What's the idea, Johnny?"

"You wasn't coming." Lacey's son was sobbing, now, the tears flooding Jesse's buckskins. "You said you was coming and when I looked, you wasn't. I got scared, Jesse. Honest Injun, *wowicake*. I'm sorry, Jesse. I—"

Jesse gritted his teeth. "Hit the dirt in there!" he yelled, shoving Johnny flat on his face between two jutting boulders. "If you so much as twitch, I'll knock your cussed head off!"

Without waiting to see his command obeyed, the mountain man threw himself over a waist-high rock and leveled on the nearest hostile, the wild-riding Blood Face. That was the greatest single shot Jesse Callahan ever made.

Not only Blood Face flew out of his saddle, but four of his braves out of theirs. And even more remarkable. Yellow Leg and two of the big-mouth warhoopers in Watonga's backside charge grabbed their bellies and lost interest in their work.

Jesse was just as confounded as the Arapaho.

Gray Bear and Elk Runner swung the remaining braves in Blood Face's bunch wide of the rocks, hightailing it for Black Coyote's riders. Pudding-proof of their panic and an almost unheard of action among Plain warriors, they left their fallen where they hit. In this case it was equal proof of their excellent judgment, too.

As they piled into Watonga's charge, checking and turning it with their warning shouts, the mystery of Jesse's great shot was blasted wide open.

Black Coyote, unable to see clearly across the rocks, missed the loss of Blood Face and the four braves, had seen Yellow Leg grab his middle, but figured that for the work of the hidden Tokeya. Jesse had seen the braves go down with no idea what sent them, had assumed that wild lead from Watonga's bucks had done the damage. The rag and tag of the galloping Indian pack, on both sides of the charge, simply had no idea what had hit them.

Watonga, Gray Bear, Elk Runner and surviving company now got the second installment of Tokeya Sha's Holy Iron Miracle. It came crashing from the elevated rocky aperture of the down-canyon trailhead, the one toward the Medicine Road. And it set three more Arapaho ponies to carrying double.

The smoke of that second volley, crawling up the canyon walls, raised the curtain on as fine a natural eyeful as ever a surrounded mountain man took in. Ranging back of their granite breastworks, waving their rifles and whooping it up as woolly as any pack of braidhair hostiles, Andy Hobbs, Morgan Bates, Joplin Smith and the balance of the Chouteau & Company mule skinners hooted and catcalled the fleeing Arapaho.

Jesse slumped down on a handy rock, feeling the sudden need for something harder than a handful of hot air under

135

his seat. "All right, Johnny boy. Come on out. We got ourselves a breather." The mountain man had to grin at the puny sound of his own voice. It wobbled out weaker than a ten-day kitten. By cripes, a man had to allow that when he'd been in a tight that cozy, he knew he'd been squeezed somewhat.

And he knew more than that as soon as he'd gotten his wind and had himself a sick smile at Lacey's young one wiggling tearful and dirty-faced out of his crack in the rocks. He knew he wasn't yet home in bed. Not by forty miles and ninety-five howling-mad Arapaho.

He and Johnny were for sure in the middle of the plank. With both ends sawed off. The Arapaho couldn't get at them without running the ambushing teamster's fire. The skinners couldn't get out to relieve them without exposing themselves to the rifles of Black Coyote's raiders. And both sides counted plenty of center shots in their ranks. When a man faced up to it, the Indians still had the top hand on the coup-stick handle.

In the mountain man's working mind, the fact that Andy Hobbs and the boys had gotten up from Old Gabe's so sudden meant one of two things: either they hadn't brought the powder wagon at all, or they'd brought it part-way and had to leave it down on the Medicine Road. From where Jesse squatted, cuddling Johnny and snatching looks at both trailheads between reassuring pats on the tousled red head, the whole thing looked like a clear stand-off.

Damn the luck. If Heyoka could still run he'd chance a dash for it in half a shuck. But the mare was stove. If she could walk out of the meadow bareback, let alone getting up a gallop under double-carry, it would be a mortal wonder. He had raveled the knit of their chances down this far when a commotion among the Arapaho sent his eyes following their excited pointings, swinging to the white side of the meadow.

Jesse grabbed his look and got excited right along with the hostiles.

Brother Moses!

Don't ask how that big, leatherfaced hardcase had done it. Don't question what skullwork and backbreak had gone betwixt him and Andy Hobbs and the rest of the skinners to get it done. Don't say a blessed thing. Just squat there and run your ever-loving eyes over her from her upswept prow to her hightailed stern; from her glaring white Osnaburg topsheets to her circus-red wheels! Yes man. Run your eyes plenty and then raise them to Old Man Above. Lift them to old Wakan Tanka. Thank him. *Ha ho. Woyuonihan.*

By God, Morgan Bates had done it—he'd brought him his gunpowder and his red-wheeled goddam!

If Watonga had a price, this was it. His band was out of meat and powder. And with a big herd of fat cows running around on the mesa above Portola Springs. *Wagh.* Any man in the business who'd been Sioux-coached and couldn't make a trade out of this tangle deserved to have his hair hoisted.

On his side of the meadow, Watonga was digging in, spreading his best shots behind the rocks flanking the up-canyon trailhead covering Jesse's hole-up as close as the skinners had it covered from their side. If it was going to be a seige the wily Arapaho was ready for it. He might be low on powder and lead, but he had a mort more of men and time than the whites.

Among their rocks, the skinners were imitating the chief's moves, shifting their individual vantage points to improve their rifle command of the trapped mountain man's cover. It was Jesse Callahan's move.

Cupping his hands, he bellowed across the meadow. "Hi there, Andy. Can you hear me?"

Jesse had a baritone halfway between a colicky boar pig and a sorethroat bullfrog. Apparently it was more than adequate, the bearded wagonmaster bellowing right back that if a couple of old North Trail hands like Jesse Callahan and A. J. Hobbs couldn't make themselves heard over two hundred yards of open meadow, they were in the wrong business. What did Mr. Callahan have on his bright young mind this bracing summer afternoon? And how would he like to hear that Mr. Hobbs had managed to bring along the whole original load of Du Pont intact?

Jesse let the thrill of that spread his rare grin about four more teeth before calling back, "All right. Fine. Now, listen. Hold her down and watch your words. Old Blackface over there, and some of his top haircutters, they catch a little white chin music." The mountain man tried using words that wouldn't likely fit into the bobtail English primer of Watonga prairie education, hoped he was getting the idea across to Andy Hobbs. "And they ain't exactly got their thumbs in their ears. You get me?"

"Like as not, little man. Can you hear this all right?"

"Just right. All set now. Watch your talk."

"I said I got you, boy. What you aim to pull? Straight trade?"

"Straight trade," the mountain man echoed him. "The Pittsburgh and Du Pont for me and the kid. What you say?"

"Bad medicine, Jesse." The old man's voice was quick with worry. "What's to keep them from accepting the swindle and then crossing us double? They got us ten to one and nobody never got fat swallowing no Injun eye-wash. I'm spooked at just giving them the Du Pont right out."

The moment Jesse had seen the powder wagon, his mind had started turning on how best to use it. When he had set out after the Arapaho, things had been a mite different. He had offhand thought that if he could bring the wagon up to the red camp on a peaceful-palaver basis, with a reinforced party of whites to back the talk up, he could trade them out of the kid with nobody getting hurt on either side.

But that was before a lot of things.

It was before he'd had to kill Ousta and carve up Watonga. It was before he could have known that when Andy Hobbs got the wagons to Fort Bridger, he would find Bridger and the other mountain men usually around the place absent from the fort and scattered God knew where. And before anybody but the old white warrior himself could have known that Old Gabe had changed his whole plan about trying to stand off Brigham Young's Danites from within the fort. Had decided to cut the timber and not be home when the Saints dropped in.

Now, hesitating, Jesse knew Andy Hobbs was plenty solid in his doubts at turning the powder over to the unstable red men. Knew also that he, Jesse, was up against a moral decision that spelled murder.

The mountain man made that decision the way he had to. Without thinking about the dirty side of it. Keeping his mind on Lacey O'Mara's kid and the dozen white men with Andy Hobbs and Morgan Bates. And keeping it on Jesse Callahan's own tender, snow-white hide.

Somebody was going to get hurt now.

Watonga had taken too much loss of face off of this particular bunch of *Wasicun* goddam drivers to let them go clean free following a peaceful trade. That was the way Andy Hobbs had it figured and he likely had it figured right. On top of that general debt, you add what Jesse had handed the giant Arapaho on his own personal account and you had a sum that toted up way too heavy for a white man to look for a steve-even trade from a red one.

Across the meadow Andy Hobbs, waiting nervously on Jesse's long silence, sang out. "Hello, Jesse. What's amiss, boy? I said I was plumb against just giving them the Du Pont clean out. Did you hear me?"

"I heard you." The mountain man's voice came quick, now, the snap and hop of it telling a decision hastily made but finally meant. "And you needn't be skittery about giving them the powder. Not the way I'm aiming to give it to them, old salt."

"What you mean? You said 'straight trade,' didn't you?"

"I'm changing that. I ain't saying it no more. You was right. We can't chance it."

"What you saying, now?"

"Straight *Injun* trade."

"Where's the difference?"

"I said 'straight *Injun*,' old hoss. You got that? We ain't trading with Old Gabe or Charley Bent, you know. Them's red Injuns over there. The whole thing's gummed up, Andy. This ain't just the ideal swap I had in mind when I took out after these sons. They got us spread so far over the barrel our bottoms are pointing sunhigh. Give one chance, the way they're gingered up now, they'd snatch the Du Pont and half our hair along with it. Brush up, Andrew!"

"Leave off the sass." The wagonmaster's yell was heating up with tension. "We ain't got all autumn here. How you aiming to trade?"

"We're trading red now. Red-style. Injun honor—" The mountain man dropped his call-back as low as he could.

"How's that again—?" Andy Hobb's voice dropped, too, now.

"*Long promise—short fuse!*" Jesse used the old frontier phrase covering the white man's belly-low opinion of his red brother's given word.

"Whoa, Nellie!" The implication in the mountain man's answer hit the old man suddenly. "You can't do that, boy. It ain't civilized—"

"I ain't, neither," barked Jesse. "Now, get ahold of Morgan and ask him did he bring that coil of touch-off medicine along. And get a move on, old hoss."

Jesse could see the oldster duck away from his rock, slide quickly back and around the far side of the Pittsburgh, go to palavering with the tall Missourian. Shortly, the boss skinner slid back along the far side of the wagon and went to rummaging in the seatbox. He was back with Andy Hobbs in a moment and the two went into another discussion. Apparently something was amiss. Either that, or Jesse was getting a mite jumpy. To the cotton-mouthed mountain man the silent seconds of the wait seemed to drag their feet louder than bone-dry brakes on a sun-blistered wagon wheel. Then, just as he was about to consign Morgan Bates and his misfire memory to the devil's hottest stovehole, the palaver broke up and old Andy doubled over for the quick scuttle back to his outpost. Once more safely behind his forward rock, the wagonmaster took up his interrupted conversation with the quietly cursing Jesse.

"Feast your peepers on her, boy! Fifty feet of the best even-burning fuse ever twisted. Morgan says you can clip it anywheres from twenty seconds to ten minutes!" With his tight-voiced call, the old man arm-waved the stiff coil of shining black loops.

Jesse let his breath go. Man! Sometimes a Minniconjou like him played in pure outhouse luck. Old Morgan hadn't let him down. Now—! With the breaking off of the thought, his long arm was returning Andy Hobbs's wave. "God bless that Missouri redneck for me, Andy. Happen his touch-off medicine works for us, I'll buy him four hundred yards of the stuff for free. Set tight, boys. Here goes for the dicker with old lumpjaw."

"Take your time," the old man hollered, acidly. "It's your red wagon!"

Jesse went down back of the rocks muttering and shaking his head.

"What's the matter, Jesse?" Johnny O'Mara's thin voice piped up, worriedly. "Ain't we going to get away after all? Gosh, I thought we was saved!"

"Shut up, boy. We're all right. I just got to have me a minute to think. You keep quiet and lay low."

With fifteen seconds of his minute unused, the mountain man stood up, jaw set, eyes narrowed nearly shut. While the crouching boy stared, fascinated, he picked up his Hawken, straightened his shoulders, and stepped slowly and deliberately into the open meadow on Watonga's side of the rockpile.

Ten long, measured strides, rifle held butt and barrel high over his head. Ten strides counted off by the growling wave of deep *hunhunhes** that rose up among the watching Arapaho. Then he stopped, held the rifle toward the hostiles, bent forward to place it on the ground. When he straightened, his hands were held shoulder-high, empty palms out, toward the Indians.

It was the Peace sign—*Woklota Wa Yaka Cola*—by Prairie protocol it could not be ignored.**

Watonga walked his pony three lengths out in front of his hidden braves. His deep voice came rolling across to Jesse, but it came without the outward palm. It came with the War Sign. With the chief's lowered hands firmly full of loaded rifle.

"What does Tokeya Sha want of Watonga? Why does he use the Holy Sign?"

Jesse let him have it, quick. The afternoon shadows were already high on the canyon walls, creeping higher by the minute. Time was running out. The mountain man's voice carried to the scowling savage, the measured Sioux cadences rolling dramatically.

Hau, kola. Hau, tahunsa. Would the great Arapaho chief accept the gift of the red-wheeled goddam with its original load of *Big Hmunha* intact? Exactly as Brigham Chief had promised it to him? Would he take the twenty-four cases of *Wasicun* gunpowder in exchange for the Courtesy Giving of Tokeya Sha and little Ya Slo to the goddam drivers from Big Throat's fort? Would Watonga do that?

The chief hesitated. Wheeled his pony, suddenly. Rode back into the cedars without a word in answer to Jesse's wheedling offer.

Five minutes passed, every last one of them sweat-damp enough to wilt the starch out of six Sunday shirts. Jesse, standing alone in the meadow, knew he was holding the biggest breath he had ever taken.

Watonga came back abruptly and black-browed as he had left.

He-hau, would Black Coyote accept the white goddam guide's crawling surrender? Would he accept the *Wasicun's* craven powder offer? *Hau*, he might do just that. Providing.

---

* A sound of vast approval, or for the welcoming of a tremendously respected person. In this case a rare tribute to the advancing white man's courage.
** The Holy Motto engraved on the Sacred Pipe of Peace of the Sioux Nation. Its use declared an inviolable truce.

Providing that he, Watonga, could inspect the goddam before accepting. That was flat, *nohetto*.

The mountain man let his breath out that loud he thought maybe the chief could have heard it, two hundred yards across the meadow.

Wagh, of course Watonga could inspect the gift. Did Black Coyote think Tokeya Sha would play him false? Lie to him? Give him short measure?

Watonga growled that he thought just that. But, *iho*, no matter. He would come in, anyway. If he liked the looks of the powder, a deal might be made. After all, Ousta was gone. There was no one to care for Ya Slo. And did not the red-haired goddam guide admit that by losing the powder to Watonga he was letting Black Coyote count the biggest coup of all? Did the Fox admit that? That the Coyote was his master?

Aii-eee! Jesse signaled his entire agreement. He was proud to admit it. It was a great honour to be beaten by a real chief like Black Coyote. *Woyuonihan. Hunhunhe.* Watonga was all man. Much more than Tokeya, the Minniconjou. Would he, then, now come in and inspect the Fox's surrender gift?

Hau, Watonga would do that. And he'd bring his chiefs along, too. He would bring Elk Runner and Gray Bear.

H'g'un, that was fine. But why bring his friends? Tokeya had no friends. Tokeya was alone, out there. Did Watonga fear to come alone to meet him? Was that the way it was?

Wagh! Iho! Never! Watonga's heart was big, like a bear's. He was coming. By Man Above he was coming, now. All by himself!

Waste, good. Tokeya would have the Old One, Big Throat's Wagon Chief, drive the red-wheeled goddam to mid-meadow. He would have the Wagon Chief to make all his men come out and stand in the open so that Watonga could see none of them were hiding in the goddam. Now, would Watonga have all his warriors ride into the grass a ways? Not far. Just a little ways. Just so the *Wasicun* could see that none of them were going around the meadow while the talk was made?

He-hau, of course. *Woyuonihan.* Black Coyote would do that. It was only common courtesy.

Waste, all was agreed, then?

Hau, all was agreed.

Jesse yelled the deal over to Andy Hobbs while Watonga

was arranging his warriors. The old man signaled his understanding, began unhooking half of the sixteen mules which had dragged the five-thousand-pound freighter up a canyon God had built to give a two-horse surrey a headache. When he was ready he made his final yell.

"How about the *Injun* part of it, boy?"

"Five foot long. And stuff it down your shirt front," Jesse echoed back. "And don't forget your tinderbox—!"

The packed ranks of Watonga's followers sat in slit-eyed silence as their chief rode out to meet the red-wheeled goddam. In mid-meadow Jesse and Andy Hobbs stood waiting, the Pittsburgh parked and rein-wrapped, the mules standing quietly.

Black Coyote rode past them without a word or look, tied his pony to the rear wheel, clambered into the sheeted Pittsburgh. He was back out in three breaths—three breaths in which one tinderbox and five feet of blackpowder fuse got from one *Wasicun's* shirt front to another's.

"How'd you find it, chief? You savvy, powder all there? *Waste*, good?" Andy Hobb's scraggly beard bobbed with the rapid questions.

"*Waste.* Powder all there. *Wiksemna nunpa dopa.* Two times ten and four. Watonga says it."

"You betcha!" the feisty beard bobbed again. "Nary a danged drachm short. Twenty-four kegs, twenty-five pounds to the keg. Six hundred pounds to the damn ounce, of the best by-God powder Du Pont ever built!"

The towering Arapaho nodded. "Good. Watonga trades. You leave powder, take boy. Get out, now. Watonga come fast, bring warriors, take powder. You leave powder on ground, take goddam. *Nohetto.*"

Jesse stood dumb as a lightning-struck ox. God Almighty, now what? Leave the powder on the ground? *Aii-eee!* There was one to twist a man's thoughts around. A real cute one. He'd sure never foresighted that idea.

Watonga sensed the mountain man's hesitation, the burr of his suspicion showing its quick bristle in his demand. "How goes it, Tokeya?" He fell back into Jesse's Sioux tongue. "I smell something. And there's no wind—"

"Of course—!" It was a wild shot, and the only one open to the floundering mountain man. "Tokeya is a fool. You smell his bad judgment. It doesn't take a wind to smell a *heyoka.* I had not seen this softness in Watonga's nature, that's all."

143

"*Softness?*" the chief's scowl clouded up black as a summer cloud. "Tokeya speaks of softness, how is that?"

"Oh, nothing. Nothing at all." Jesse kept the shrug as insultingly careless as he could. "It was not in my mind to think Watonga would weaken thus toward an enemy. Aye, to think of it! Letting Tokeya make away with a thing which has been such a curse to you. Naturally, I thought it would be taken and burned. To be made to count as a real coup. Especially since the chief must remember that I heard him say to Ousta that it was the curse of his life. And that he would rather count a coup on it than to eat fat cow all winter. Ah, well. Tokeya is grateful. Watonga is as graceful as a woman. *Ha ho!*"

"Do not thank me—" The chief's huge jaw chopped the ugly words short. "It is nothing. Thank your big mouth for what you hear now. Watonga did *not* remember that you heard that curse. Leave it there. Right where it is. With all the powder in it!" With the angry demand, the Arapaho swung his four-foot skullclub and with a great shout of "*Onhey!*"* smote the side boards of the Pittsburgh a thunderous clout.

"Now, wait—! Watonga said I could take the goddam—" Jesse made the objection hesitantly, hoping he wasn't overputting it.

He wasn't.

"Leave the goddam! That's the way it will be now," snapped Watonga. "*Nohetto!*"

"*Nohetto,*" sighed Jesse, bowing regretfully to the superior power of the hulking raider. "Perhaps in time Tokeya will learn that Watonga is all the man he looks."

"I am going," was all the Arapaho said, turning his roan pony with the words.

"Wait—!" Jesse's hand gestured quickly. "You have counted the powder. I have not. Would Tokeya Sha give a gift not knowing it was all there, as his word was given on it?"

"*Woyuonihan,*" grunted Watonga, waving his hand haughtily. "Be quick about it. I honor you."

Jesse was inside the wagon before the chief's words were well out. Once there, he found the sheeted dimness too uncertain for an honest count. Surely there could be no objec-

* The word shouted when the first coup is struck on an enemy, literally, "I kill him first!"

144

tion to striking a little light with Andy Hobbs's tinderbox. Nor to getting that damn stiff fuse out of his shirt front, so it wouldn't chafe him out of being absolutely sure Black Coyote got everything that had been promised him.

A man had to have things just so, in a close deal like this one.

When the mountain man crawled back out of the Pittsburgh, a sharp eye might have wondered what he was in such a mortal hurry about it. And about the way he talked when he did get out.

But Watonga's beady orbs were busy with pleasanter prospects. *Ha! Iho!* How blind were these white antelopes? Oh, sure. Let them give him the goddam full of powder. Let them leave it there and go running for their rocks. *Hau*, let them go. It was a long way to Big Throat's fort. And did they know about the hidden way to climb out of Little Chief's Gorge, back there where the grass grew wide among the cedars? The way that would let a fast pony get back to the Medicine Road well ahead of any band of *Wasicun* goddam drivers traveling down the main canyon trail? Did they know that? About that secret way Watonga would have sent warriors to cut off Tokeya and Ya Slo, had he not known he could catch them so easily without doing so?

Iho, indeed. Here was a trade that wasn't done yet.

"All right," Jesse's hurrying words cut the chief's *Wickmunke Dreaming* short. "It's all there. We have traded."

"*Ni'inaei*, good hunting," grinned Watonga, making rare use of the Arapaho phrase in place of the generally spoken Sioux. "*H'g'un!*"

With the courage-shout, the fleeting grin died stillborn, leaving Black Coyote's face as blank as a basalt rock. The obsidian glitter of his tiny eyes held Jesse while a slow man might have counted five. Then he was gone, his blue roan gelding digging on a dead gallop toward the waiting warriors.

"Leg it, Andy!" The mountain man's shout was wasted back of the dust puffs already being sent up by the wagonmaster's thudding boots. As the old man looked back, Jesse waved him on. "Go on, leg it! I'll get the boy."

Johnny, hearing the yell, scudded from the rocks, heading for Jesse. The mountain man scooped him up on the run, legged it for the cheering teamsters as tight as his long shanks would churn.

Johnny O'Mara wasn't the only one to respond to Jesse's

shout. As the mountain man grabbed the boy and ran for the skinners, a forlorn, dusk-gray ghost tottered out of the rocks to follow along in a stumbling trot. Heyoka, the knock-kneed clown, wasn't aiming to be left behind. Not while she could still see, and had breath left in her to go after the red-haired *Wasicun*.

By the time Jesse and Johnny reached the down-canyon rocks, the Arapaho had swarmed across the meadow, surrounding the Pittsburgh and boosting Watonga up onto the wagonbox.

And there, mounted triumphantly on the driver's seat of Tokeya's Sha red-wheeled goddam, all six feet three of him standing black and stark against the white Osnaburg backdrop, Watonga, War Chief of the Wind River Arapaho, made his departing oration of acceptance. Then, his faithful crowding the wagon-hubs as close as their scrawny ponies could jam, he seized the unfamiliar wrap of the multiple reins, started the *Wasicun's* Fear Gift uncertainly across the meadow. His final, jeering shout at Jesse reminded the cowardly mountain man that in the end it was he, Watonga, who had proved the better man, he, Black Coyote, who was finally going to get what was rightly coming to him.

Which he did. Six seconds and one inch of fuse later.

The twenty-four kegs of powder made a nice salute to the chief's phenomenal gift of prophecy. Choice cuts of Chouteau & Company mule, Indian pony and male Arapaho, mingled with a fine selection of oak spokes, hickory whiffletrees and draw-iron wheel rims, scattered skyward. The clapping thunder of the explosion rocketed back and forth between the narrow canyon walls fit to split a man's earskins clean across.

Jesse shook his head to get the ringing out of it, peered intently under the rolling cloud of powder smoke. At first glance, he counted eight sprawling braves who were already pounding their stiffening rears up the misty trail to *Wanagi Yata*, another limping three dozen who would carry pieces of Pittsburgh and pepperings of Jesse Callahan's Du Pont powder buried under their smoking hides for all their days short of The Place Where The Souls Gather.

One membrous figure, tottering, waveringly toward the far edge of the meadow, brought a strange leap to the watching mountain man's heart.

As will sometimes unaccountably happen with those who are the very closest to the source of the explosion, Black Coyote had miraculously survived. Blown skyhigh, dumped

146

bareskin-naked into the spiny clutch of an early berry bush, the old warrior had come out of it alive. His panicky braves, unfamiliar with gunpowder in larger than buffalo hornsfuls, were hustling him aboard a squealing, wild-eyed pony, were cutting out of the meadow for all they were worth, jamming and packing the entrance of the up-canyon trailhead.

Watching the route, Jesse yelled along the line of bead-drawing skinners. "Hold your fire, boys! They've had it. No use kicking them when they're done and down. Leave the buzzards go."

The last of the braves were crowding through the far trailhead, the still reeling Watonga supported among them. The mountain man's rare grin cracked the dirty granite of his jaw.

Sure, leave the red sons go. He had set out long days ago to skin that arrogant scut of a Watonga, true. But what with his Arapaho hide still smoking from its twenty-four-keg, gunpowder cure, and his hog-size Indian ego blistered worse than a lapful of hot grease, the haughty chief's peltry was hardly worth the sweat it would take a man to peel it off to him.

Not to Jesse Callahan it wasn't, anyhow.

Jesse was a man who never messed with any skin that wasn't plumb prime. Leastways, never killed for one that wasn't.

8. FORT BRIDGER

It was a loud-talking band of Chouteau & Company skinners that rode the shadowed reaches of Carson's Canyon downtrail of Rockpile Meadow that early fall evening.

Heading them, pert as a peafowl, astride a captured calico pony, rode young Johnny O'Mara, proudly flanked by Morgan Bates and Joplin Smith.

The two skinners had their horses trapped with feathered Arapaho headstalls, their persons dripping buckskins and beadwork, while behind them scarce a man in the outfit failed to sport some spoils of Jesse's hard-driven *Indian trade*. A horsehair-tassled buffalo lance here. A heron-plumed coupstick there. And here and there a sprinkling of squat Arapaho war bows, beautifully worked elkhead quivers, tooled parfleches, quilled moccasins, bearclaw necklaces, buffalo horn and halfskull headdresses, stone pipes, handmade skinning knives and scarlet Three Point Nor'west blankets: together, the whole gaudy ragtassel of peeled-off Plains Indian war dress which told the story of ten naked braves silent amid a lonely pile of meadow rocks.

Behind Johnny and his jubilant escort, Jesse and Andy Hobbs rode in wordless quiet.

Glancing at his companion, the old man marked the brooding, narrow-eyed stare, the wide clamp of the Sioux mouth, knew the gaunt mountain man was mind-riding the backtrail.

"You couldn't help it, Jesse." The words came as soft as the touch of the weathered paw on his companion's knee. "You had to think of the kid first."

"Sure," the answer came after a short silence, "I reckon. But it shames me all the same, Andy. I feel mortal bad about it, somehow."

"Ain't no call for you to feel thataway, young un. They was hostile Injuns, and trail raiders to boot. And any red

148

bunch that works the Oregon Road knows what to expect when they wipe out a settler band and carry off a young un."

Jesse nodded. "Yeah, Andy, I allow you're right. Watonga sure knowed what he was asking for when he hit them emigrants and hoisted Lacey's kid. Not to mention what the squaw did to the baby."

The wagonmaster lifted his hand from the mountain man's knee and placed it gently on his shoulder. "Matter of fact, Jesse, I allow you done the whole Medicine Road traffic a powerful turn. Jim Bridger has had hisself twenty years' hard work building a peaceful trade with Washakie and them friendly Snakes of his'n. Him and the other traders sure can't afford to have these here wild northern cousins filtering down getting the friendlies riled up again. And you done put a sharp-hard stop to any such notions they might of had, with that powder trade just now."

"Happen I hope you're right, Andy. That was strong medicine I dosed old Black Coyote with. I'd feel a heap better to figure he had it coming to him for more'n just what he done to us."

"Well, you just figure he had, son. He had and you can tie on it. And I'll tell you how it's going to be now—

"Old Black Coyote, he's the big chief up north. So when a dozen Missouri mule skinners and one medium-size, redhead mountain man can knock the hides off'n a hundred of his top warriors three times, hand running, it's going to shrink the size of his tipi, considerable. Time he gets home with what's left of his tail tucked between his legs, every Arapaho north of the Platte is going to know there's easier ways of making a living than working the old Medicine Road.

"I allow it'll be a long, hot winter in Montany before another Arapaho chief come down to raid the Californy traffic."

"Let's hope," said Jesse despondently. "This lying and killing, red or white, don't add up to nothing but more of the same."

"—And another thing." Andy Hobbs worked ahead, patiently ignoring the mountain man. "You're square with Bridger on the powder. His Snake wife there at the fort told me Gabe's done changed his whole idee about battling Brigham for the post. Says Gabe is aiming to winter in the hills, hid out, and just leave Brigham and his Danites set in the place till spring. Figures they'll come out poorer by

149

wintering through than by fighting. Naturally, that's how come us to have all the Du Pont for your swap."

"Well, that works out slicker'n green bear grease for me." Jesse got his grin back, gradually. "Happen Gabe chooses to get generous, I can stand it. Though I reckon what with losing the powder I won't get no pay for my peltries."

"I allow you will," countered the old man quietly. "Bridger's Snake woman said she could guarantee that. She figures Old Gabe'll be so plumb tickled to hear about how you kept Brigham from getting his Saintly paws on all them supplies and turning that powder over to the hostiles, he'll give you full price for your skins and glad of the chance. You'll get your thousand dollars, Jesse."

"Andy—" the mention of the money brought other pictures than Jim Bridger and Brigham Young to the mountain man's mind, the sudden eagerness of his voice telling the nature of them, "how'd Lacey come around about the little gal? And me, and all? I had to smack her back there at Wild Hoss Bend. She was clean out'n her mind about losing the baby, and I—"

"She's all right, son," the oldster interrupted earnestly. "I talked her around to the idee the baby was done for anyways. I figure she really was, too. Don't you?"

"Sure, Andy. She had the lung fever, fatal bad."

"Well, you got yourself a real woman, there."

"Yep!" the dark-faced trapper brightened. "She's prime beaver. I can scarce wait to get to Gabe's to see her. You know, Andy, we ain't rightly had a chance to talk proper yet. I broached some purty big plans about Californy, first-off I met her. I sure hope she ain't been scared off'n them by all this crazyhead shagging around after redskins."

"She ain't, mister!" The old man wagged his head, satisfied now that he had the mountain man eased out of his dour Sioux mood. "She's hotter'n a four-peso Spanish pistol for anything that's spelled Jesse Callahan. Including his addlepate idees. And more, too," the wagonmaster played his hole card, craftily, "you ain't going to have to wait to get to Gabe's to find it out, neither!"

As he spoke and before Jesse could reply, the canyon ahead flared out for its confluence with the Medicine Road. The sloping decline of the canyon floor spread wide and clear in the late twilight, letting Jesse see the bright beacons of the cookfires in the main trail ahead.

"That's our base camp, Jesse. Some of Gabe's Snakes, with

our spare stock and supplies. We brung everything we might need to run you and the boy clean to Canady. I allow you can see what else we brung you—"

Jesse had dug his heels in before the wagonmaster finished talking. His mount shot up through the loose-riding mule skinners, swung in between Morgan Bates and Joplin, swerved up alongside Johnny's spotted pony.

He made a one-arm snatch of the surprised boy, scooping him off the pony and onto the pounding withers of his own mount, all to the startling tune of a long-drawn Minniconjou yell.

Following his careening ride toward the base camp, the laughing teamsters saw the tiny figure waiting against the flare of the distant cookfires. It was a long, dim ways, but a man couldn't miss those lines. Especially when what made them was running and waving right at him. There was something about the way some women moved that would hit a man's mind and jump his heart as long as his blood was pumping and as far as his eyes could reach.

And this was *some* woman!

"It's Mom! It's my mom!" Johnny was laughing and crying and waving all at the same time. The mountain man's response to the boy's excitement was a sound precious few humans had ever heard—Jesse Callahan laughing out loud.

"*Hii-yeee-hahh!* Shout it out, boy! It ain't your Aunt Harriet!"

Seconds later, one indignant, borrowed Arapaho horse was getting his haunchhide burned off on the dry granite of the Medicine Road, and little Johnny O'Mara was that wrapped up in a flying smother of mother hugs and kisses, he couldn't get his wind to whistle.

Jesse legged it slowly down off his eared-back mount, stepped toward Lacey and the boy. "Don't be a hawg, son." The words were for Johnny but the blue-dark eyes behind them went into the upswinging, wide gaze of Lacey O'Mara. "Leave some for your old man—"

He stood with the tear-wet of her thick lashes locked into the hollow of his shoulder, his lean face, flushed and fever-dark, buried in the warmth of her hair. "It's all right, Lacey, honey. Everything's all right, now. We got our young un back and the three of us are going to make it to Californy before snow flies. And if they want, we'll take your Kansas folks along, too.

"Listen to me, honey. We got the world in a ju

Lacey, gal—" His deep growl dropped softer than new snow. "There ain't nobody but God Almighty, hisself, ever going to pull the stopper on us again."

The emigrant girl nodded, the silent, upturned starshine of her blue eyes returning all the answer the mountain man would ever need. She took his great paw in one slim hand, reaching the other to the clinging Johnny, the three of them moving slowly toward the welcoming wink of the campfires. Their shoulder-close silhouettes loomed briefly against the flickering rose glow of the camp light—long enough to limn the final, long-sighed nestle of the golden-haired head into the broad haven of the scout's shoulder, the lean-reaching encirclement of the willing waist by the buckskinned arm—they were lost in the deepening well of the ground shadows.

Back of the crowding hills, a prowling sage wolf lifted the plaintive opening call for the early evening, prairie overture. The lilting sadness of his invitation was echoed from beyond the growing twilight by a second and a third dolorously compelling reply. Downtrail, the haunting, powdersoft whip of the awakening poorwills joined the building chorus, the querulous pee-weet, pee-weet of a complaining plover counterpointing their melody. To the north, far and faint from beyond the brooding stillness of Rockpile Meadow, drifted the minor chord completion—the long-held, sob-lonely hunting song of the Buffalo Wolf.

The nightdark came down heavy as the trail-weary skinners kneed their ambling mounts along the path of Jesse's campward gallop. The wiry little horses picked up to a shuffle trot, moving eagerly toward the distant cheer of the fire-blooms.

Through the settling dust of their passing, the last member of the returning caravan plodded unsteadily.

There was enough light to make out her pop-eyed, outsized head, her wobbling cowhocks and stiff-splinted knees, even the ugly, smoke-dirty color of her lather-stained hide.

And then there was just enough light left over to mark the memorable snowflash of Watonga's eight-foot, eagle-feather bonnet where it swung and jolted in tired and final across the bony withers of Heyoka, The Clown—all left to signal and dignify the trail's end skinning of